PRAISE FOR *UP IN THE MAIN HOUSE*

"Savage short stories…where characters can sniff out vulnerabilities a mile away. A collection that stands out just as much for what remains lurking in the dark as what lies dissected and exposed in full view."
—*Kirkus Reviews*

"Nadeem Zaman's stories are rich with the drama, small victories, and heart-rending choices of ordinary lives. The characters are evocatively drawn, jumping off the page into my imagination…This collection is filled with surprises and illuminations, powerfully capturing the lives of some of Dhaka's citizens in ways that will stay with you."
—**Sharbari Zohra Ahmed, author of** *The Ocean of Mrs Nagai: Stories*

"In prose and manners at times reminiscent of V.S. Naipaul or John Updike, Nadeem Zaman's *Up in the Main House & Other Stories* artfully tracks the progress and set-backs of middle class Bangladeshis contending with the pressures of social change… Zaman meticulously textures a portrait of Dhaka that is somehow at once shattering and loving."
—**Jerry Gabriel, author of** *Drowned Boy* **and** *The Let Go*

"A remarkable collection of stories that captures, in dense, atomic detail, the warp and weft of Dhaka's tapestry of lives. Zaman's work invites comparison to Arvind Adiga's *White Tiger* for its resolute, unsentimental depiction of the frozen web of hierarchical power and societal expectations in which we find ourselves trapped, whether we are master or servant, hero or villain."—**Arif Anwar, author of** *The Storm*

UP IN THE MAIN HOUSE
& Other Stories

UP IN THE MAIN HOUSE

& Other Stories

NADEEM ZAMAN

The Unnamed Press
Los Angeles, CA

AN UNNAMED PRESS BOOK

www.unnamedpress.com

Unnamed Press, and the colophon, are registered trademarks of Unnamed Media LLC.

Library of Congress Control Number: 2019030045.

ISBN: 978-1944700-980

Earlier versions of the following stories appeared in: *Roanoke Review* ("Adulteress"), *East Bay Review* ("Dual Income"), and *The Milo Review* ("The Forced Witness").

Cover artwork by Marisol Ortega
Designed & typeset by Jaya Nicely
Distributed by Publishers Group West
Manufactured in the United States of America

First Edition

1 3 5 7 9 10 8 6 4 2

This book was published in partnership with Bengal Lights Books (BLB), Dhaka, Bangladesh.

www.bengallights.com

Table of Contents

UP IN THE MAIN HOUSE
& Other Stories

Up in the Main House

Kabir let out a long onion belch and struck a match to his beedi. His wife was a much better cook when the master and mistress were gone, because the high-strung hag wasn't around to be a constant harassment when Anwara was preparing a meal: too much salt, more water, more water, more water, even in boiling water more water, stir the pot nonstop, all the pots, at the same time, watch for burning, stop daydreaming, don't dream at all, not even while asleep. Now that Kabir and Anwara had the house to themselves for a week—except for Ramzan, the night guard, who arrived for his shift at sundown and left after taking tea and morning prayers—Kabir could finally enjoy his wife's cooking.

The inky mass of the night sky allowed for a cluster of stars over the roof of the neighbor's house to blink and pulse. There was the phantom glow of an unseen moon. On the long bench in front of the garage, Kabir sat under the balcony of the servants' quarters, smoking, wondering what his wife was doing inside the house. From the far end of the driveway, by the main gates of the house floated Ramzan's humming, tunes that rose and fell in pitch, paused, resumed, as if a whole album of songs known only to the night guard was spinning on a turntable inside his head.

Kabir finished the beedi, yawned, stretched luxuriously like a cat and pulled himself to his feet, feeling the weight of his dinner as he did so. He walked down the driveway toward the front of the mostly darkened house. The lights of the master bedroom remained on, blushing the bank of curtained windows, which meant that she'd nearly finished her rounds. Each night, Anwara would begin with the lights on in every room, and Kabir could mark the progress of her work by the overall darkness of the house.

"My knees are getting stiff, young blood," Ramzan said, shifting in his chair. Kabir had walked within a foot of the night guard on his perch. "And my elbows. Neck too, especially after a night's sleep. Means winter's here, no?"

"Winter is still two months away," said Kabir.

"Who can tell any more these days? When I was a child, we knew the seasons, how long they would last, how long before the next one. Now it's all one in the same day."

"Things feel different in the village than out here in the city," said Kabir.

"I can tell from the scent in the air that your missus has cooked a lord's fare."

Kabir laughed and gave the guard's shoulder a light slap. "That nose of yours. The rest of you will get old and hurt and break, but not that nose. Yes, she cooked to her heart's desire, and I ate it the same way. She prepared a plate for you. It's on the counter next to the stove. Get some of that grease in your system to keep those stiff joints working."

"Young blood, I would happily give away my useless old testicles to the pie dogs to be able to eat like that again," said Ramzan sadly. "I'll stick with my bread and milk, and tea."

Ramzan's head shifted upward. He smiled. "Look, look. There's something for you up in the window."

Anwara was at the window positioned between a parting in the curtains, backlit like a scene from a movie. Even in silhouette, Kabir couldn't get enough of her. It wasn't a young marriage either. Their childless union was twelve years old, but neither remembered when they had stopped enjoying each other for the futile task of making babies and continued only to enjoy each other for the sake of it, with a vigor that, time and again through the years, left them astounded.

The old night guard pinched a smile up at Anwara, which she most likely missed. "Go, go, young blood. Everything good in life is yours." He gave Kabir a wink, lowered his chin to his chest, and picked up his humming.

"What are you doing?" Kabir said from the door of the master bedroom.

"This looks better on me than it would ever on that skeleton of a woman," said Anwara. She was standing in front of the full-size mirror next to the dressing table, with her back to Kabir, modeling for herself. "Tell me you think so."

"I think, my dear, that you're slightly more out of your mind than usual," Kabir laughed.

"You know exactly how beautiful I look, my fool, how much you desire me in this. Say whatever else you wish."

"I say it's time for you to step out of fantasies and get into bed with your man."

Anwara regarded herself in the mirror. "You're a fed and fattened brute right now," she said. "I've cleaned myself and scented my body."

Kabir entered the room and approached his wife, and within a foot from her was struck by a hit of perfume that had him sneezing. Anwara backed away from him, moving toward the dressing table where she sat down on the small bench, lifted a silver-plated brush, and began drawing it through her hair. Teary-eyed, Kabir moved behind her. The two of them were framed in the oval mirror of the dressing table like a formal portrait, the pristine lady and her unkempt charmer.

"Let's go," he said. "You've had your fun."

"And now you want yours." Her eyes met his in the mirror.

Kabir grinned, and placed his hands on her shoulders, which made her flinch and brush them off like dirt.

"Have you gone seriously mad?" said Kabir.

"Only way you get to touch me is by cleaning yourself and coming to me like a real man," said Anwara.

"I'll show you a real man."

"Go, if you don't want me to lock you out of this room for the whole night."

"Go where?"

"In there," Anwara pointed toward the bathroom.

"You want me to do what in there?"

"Make yourself ready and worthy of me," said Anwara, haughtily coy, checking his face in the mirror with a quick dart of her eyes, and returning to brushing her hair.

"Woman, for God's sake," said Kabir. "You'll get us both murdered. Take off that ridiculous dress and put it away as you found it. And come to your senses at least if you won't come to bed."

"You can go to your bed anytime you wish," said Anwara, letting loose hair from her fingertips float to the ground. "My bed is right back there."

"This is madness," Kabir half-turned away, speaking as if to a third person in the room, there to mediate the argument.

Anwara began humming. Hers was a disconnected set of whinnies, far more confusing in their arrangement than even old Ramzan's compositions. She was exactly as she believed herself to be at that moment, a privileged, pampered ingénue whose graces were the envy of a thousand of her peers, whose affection would be the ultimate trophy of countless suitors, and the only thing she owed the world was to go on existing exactly as she was.

"Then you will go mad standing there," Anwara said, standing, moving around him toward the bed, while Kabir watched his wife of a dozen years with the stupefied look of one watching magic tricks. "Or find yourself back outside, down in the cold servants' quarters, keeping yourself warm." She sat at the foot of the bed, crossed her legs at the knees, leaned back on a hand, and waited for his next move.

"What do you want me to do?" he asked.

"Undress," said Anwara. "The way you like to see me undress, bit by bit, every night."

A half-smile played around her mouth while she waited. It was wide enough for Kabir to be able to see the small chip at the corner of her front upper tooth—which, to give the banshee of a mistress they worked for credit where she deserved it, would have been fixed and paid for if not for Anwara's repeated refusal—and it was enough for him to shed his clothes in a few quick moves.

Her eyes took him in like no other time he could remember. Then her head flew back and she fell on the bed, both hands covering her mouth, her unseen legs flailing under the dress making it look like someone was trying desperately to find their way out from under it. Kabir reached for his clothes pooled at his feet.

"What are you doing?" said Anwara, a new wave of laughter diffusing at the sight of Kabir reaching for his clothes. Her tone was of a child whose playmate had suddenly decided their game was no longer fun.

"You want to joke around, woman, stay here and dress up and laugh at yourself all night," said Kabir.

"Fine, I will," said Anwara. "I will stay up here every night, all week."

"What?" Kabir stopped, his shirt dangling from his hand.

"I promise you, I will," Anwara said. "All week, every night. It's up to you if you want to be let in with me."

"What if Ramzan says something?"

"He won't."

"So sure, are you?"

"Yes. He's old. He's not a fool. He's had his day."

"*If* he does, then..."

"That is an 'if' with a heavy price for you to pay," Anwara said.

"You talk like one of those shrewd old generals planning a coup," said Kabir. "My father worked for one, remember? I lived in a house where people came and went talking like that day and night."

"Am I really that cunning?" Anwara sat up. "I always thought you took me to be your dull little wife, here to cook for you and fuck you."

"God defend my soul, woman," said Kabir. "What did you feed yourself that you're talking like this?"

"It's the dress," said Anwara. "Having the bitch's clothes on me has given me her tongue. I knew I felt different the moment the fabric touched my skin. I like it. I get why she loves so much being the way she is, pushing her way through everyone and everything, not leaving any chance for someone to push her around."

"I push you around?" said Kabir.

"Yes. All the time."

"Is that why I'm standing naked here like a monkey at your command?"

A car passed along the street, inching its way past the house, its headlights suddenly illuminating the windows like sweeping searchlights even though the bedroom was already sufficiently lit.

"This is foolish," Kabir said, stepping into his shorts, and beginning to pull up his pants.

"I hope you have a nice, warm night, husband," said Anwara. "I know I will." She pulled back a corner of the thick blanket and wrapped it over her chest. "For a whole week."

"You want to be out of your mind, then be out of your mind," said Kabir, pulling his shirt over his head. "Have fun with it, all by yourself." In his frustration he tugged his belt too hard, and it pinched the skin under his belly button, making him wince.

"Have many sweet dreams, my love," Anwara's voice rose from the folds of the blanket, almost a purr.

Downstairs, Kabir lit a beedi and pulled it into his lungs until he could inhale no more. Tears rose to his eyes when he finally exhaled. He began coughing, the way he had after his very first puff from his father's beedi. He stepped out onto the driveway, and cursed his hasty retreat. His damn foolish pride; that had done it. Just like it had done it countless times over the years, tightening like a vise inside him, doing no more in the end than undoing his grit to push it away, leaving him as he was now, too far gone to turn back, give in.

"What I wouldn't give for your young stomach," Ramzan said, coming out of the kitchen to the bench in front of the garage where Kabir sat smoking. "Just a little taste I took, enough I think that I've buggered myself for the rest of the night. Young blood, that woman is a precious stone."

"She's acting like one too," Kabir mumbled.

"What's that?" Ramzan cupped his ear and leaned closer.

"What's one night of pain for a good meal?" Kabir sighed.

"If you want my job, young blood, just say it. Why wish such a painful death on an old man?"

"I'm the one bringing a painful death on myself with these," Kabir held up the beedi pinched between forefinger and thumb.

"This is the third generation of this family that I've served as night guard," said Ramzan. "When I first started, young blood, I was younger than you, day and night smoking, drinking on my days off, never thinking that this body would get old and start to break." He laughed quietly with his head down, shaking. "Didn't think even once of giving it to a good woman."

Kabir regarded the main house, for a moment feeling as though he was as near to it as he would ever get again. Powers unknown to him had separated Anwara from him, irreversibly, forever, and he was condemned to spend his life shackled to this bench, steps away from the nearest entrance to the house, never to make his way back in.

"You know what I'm telling you, young blood?" Ramzan said.

"I thought you had been married," said Kabir.

"Oh, yes, sure, married I have been. Twice. Both of their souls may God rest in peace. And my sons, what stock, young blood, first time in the history of the family had anyone produced such sturdy, sharp-minded gifts. You see, I continue to be here out of one thing only, loyalty. I could have long ago had one of my boys put me up in a quiet place, and all four of them would have placed themselves at my feet day and night. That's not what I want, for them or for me. If you saw them you wouldn't think they came from two different women. Devoted brothers, loyal to the last hair on their heads. What more can I ask for in this life, young blood?"

"A stronger stomach," Kabir said, laughing.

"Yes, young blood, yes," Ramzan joined in his laughter. Ramzan's knees popped as he pushed himself to his feet.

"Okay, young blood, time for me to get back to my place. Maybe I'll see if that old crank next door wants to talk about being old, while you go take care of that little woman."

"You just want to make him crankier than he already is," Kabir motioned with his head toward the neighbor's house.

"That fool was born cranky," said Ramzan. "You know, there was once nothing around here but open space. When he and I were kids. None of these houses, none of the buildings, none of the goddamn traffic. Just space, if you can believe it about this city, where you can't turn from left to right without hitting your nose against someone's face. And foxes. Foxes everywhere. Out there in Banani Cemetery. Everywhere. Now even the place of the dead is too full."

Kabir entered the house through the front veranda, reached the stairs, and listened for any sound from above. In the tomblike stillness he could hear the pendulum of the grandfather clock in the living room marking time, and as he mounted the first step, the distant, scolding summons of a car horn.

He reached the top of the stairs, the large outer room that served as a common area and den and peeled his ears once more for sounds of his wife. There was the small hall-way to his left that led to the master bedroom. He wanted to call her name, but the darkness was dissuading.

Kabir felt the unease of someone on the cusp of break-ing an oath not to venture into certain places, do certain things, see certain people. Five minutes passed before he shook off this devotion to a silent, dark hallway that had risen in his wandering notions to heights of fealty. He was a paid employee. His work began at dawn and, on certain weekends when guests were invited for a dinner party, kept him up well past midnight, even sunrise. He was, however, no serf; he didn't serve a landlord with his life as a show of loyalty. And that was *his* wife in there, no matter whose house he was standing in.

When he pushed down on the handle it was locked. Kabir knocked. He feared she'd fallen asleep. And when she slept, she *slept*. So it had been from their first time together: their wedding night, when Kabir had entered the room his father had set up for them with a new queen-size bed, dressing table, and nightstands, only to find his bride still in her full wedding attire sprawled out on her stomach and snoring.

He knocked again and called her name. Thinking he heard stirring inside, he stood back for the door to open. Nothing happened.

"This is nonsense," he grumbled after a long minute, and rattled the handle again as if, broken down by his impatience alone, it would come unlocked. "This is too much." But he knew that short of breaking down the door, through which his wife would remain soundly sleeping, tonight he was not getting in.

He went back out to the common area. On the long cane sofa next to the small balcony that overlooked the back of the house and the servants' quarters, he stretched out and lit a beedi. He looked up at the half moon that was now visible in the sky, bright enough to illuminate his bedroom in the servants' quarters and their neatly made, perfectly empty bed.

"Young blood, it's almost eight."

Kabir was balled up in a fetal position; he turned his shoulder to roll on his back.

"And smoking inside the house," Ramzan said, bending down and pinching the half smoked beedi off the carpet. "The whole house gone up in beedi flames. Imagine how embarrassing it would be for the master and mistress. Get up, young blood, I have to go home and rest myself."

Kabir sprang up, in the process making himself dizzy.

"Your wife is already downstairs," Ramzan said, with a tired grin. "She made me my tea, and I believe she has been making breakfast for someone, although I'm not sure who." His grin widened, and he winked in the way that he always did, with both eyes.

"Was it good, sleeping by yourself?" Kabir asked, watching his wife at the kitchen sink.

"Stop hovering back there and come eat your breakfast," Anwara said without turning.

"I'm surprised that you even thought of making it," said Kabir.

"You are a child." Anwara set down the pan she had finished rinsing in the sink and dried her hands with a sodden dishtowel.

"I was just outside, you know, all night."

"I know."

"You do?"

"I know when you're within ten feet of me."

"Close enough to be spit at, too."

Anwara, in the midst of pouring tea for her husband, stopped. In her grip the kettle hovered over the cup, as she gave her husband her first serious look since the night before, moments before she had him shedding his clothes.

"I am a woman, and a lady," said Anwara, letting the tea stream back into the cup. "Maybe I should remind you of that again tonight?"

"Again tonight? One night's play isn't enough?"

"A house always needs its lady."

"And this house already has one."

"When she is not here she cannot be the lady of the house."

"I don't think she would want her servant to take over the role either."

"When she is not here, I am no one's servant."

Kabir tore off a piece of chapatti and used it to scoop up the potatoes fried in mustard oil. She could put on all the veneers she wanted to, be snide and aloof, but she had spent her morning making his favorite breakfast item, and that said enough.

Part of Kabir hoped that the master and mistress would end their trip early, as they had done numerous times in the past, and he spent his afternoon straining his ears for the slowing of cars as they passed by the house, hoping the next one would be the blaring horn he wanted to hear.

There wasn't much work for him to do, nor, for that matter, was his wife burdened with her usual daily chores. Inside and out, the house was clean, and Kabir's only other headache was to perform regular rounds of the excessively large compound. At night, though, he had never seen Ramzan walk any further than the servants' latrine as part of his patrols. In the event of an incident, both of them, separately or together, could be overpowered just as easily by one skilled intruder as by a gang of thugs. Still, Kabir made his way around the compound absentmindedly three times during the day, and by the end of the third round felt that when asked if he had kept up with his premise-checks, his answer could be honest.

Kabir went to the far edge of the lawn that wound around the house, walking in line along the flowerbeds that were separated from the grass by rows of bricks half-buried into the soil, jutting out in triangles. He found his rounds unsettling for the simple distance they created between him and the house. He felt as though he were unmoored in open waters with no wind left in his lungs or power in his body to make his way back to the distant shore. These irrational thoughts were sometimes so vivid that Kabir would have to step onto a flowerbed before his mind could accept that he wasn't about to plunge into the depths of a bottomless sea.

By the end of his last rounds the sun had all but set. Wondering about Ramzan, he opened the main gates and stepped outside. He lit a beedi, sat on the night guard's cane chair that was sturdier than any of the expensive ones in the house, and turned his attention to the bedroom window above. Once more, while the rest of the house was dark as a defunct warehouse, up in the bedroom he knew it was his wife keeping the solitary light burning.

He heard humming behind him. Out of tune, out of joint, but steady and proud. The little figure was trotting toward his nightly watch with the enthusiasm of a teenager on his way to see his girlfriend. Kabir didn't feel one way or another about work. It was something that was—that needed to be done. When it was over for the day, it was time to let go of it. He didn't understand people who were so consumed by work that they enjoyed it. For Kabir, work was banal, routine, something the body and mind were taught to do over time, through dull repetition until it was as familiar as breathing. It was when he encountered people like Ramzan that he found himself reevaluating work, trying to comprehend from which parts of it one could muster pure honest joy.

"Is that you, young blood?" said Ramzan between strains of humming.

"Not to worry. I'm not taking over your job."

Ramzan laughed softly.

"I'm not worried, young blood. But here I am, and the night is here, too. I see the light on in the bedroom again." Ramzan grinned.

"I'm going to tell her to stop," said Kabir. "Tonight."

"Why? Let her have her fun. She isn't harming anyone. Just go up there and join her. In your place, young blood, that would be my only concern."

"All these years, and I just don't understand her sometimes."

Ramzan laughed. "The day man has the capacity to understand women, that would be a true miracle on God's earth."

"So? That means we men are inferior?"

"We certainly lack some fundamental skills." Another spurt of laughter, and the night guard grew serious, sagacious. "Why else do we quarrel like mortal enemies with the only ones in our lives not tied to us by blood, but who give us their lives so unconditionally?"

"She and I don't quarrel much," said Kabir. "When we do, it's not even what you might call a quarrel anyway."

"Quarrels are the lowest forms of our consciousness. So low that we don't know who we are when we're in the midst of them."

"I didn't know you were such a thinking man."

"I'm not. My head is already hurting. I'm an old man. Now go upstairs and have some fun."

Anwara had wrapped herself in an olive-green sari bordered in gold, no blouse, leaving Kabir to wonder if a petticoat was also absent underneath. The door to the room was wide open. He found her talking to the mirror, playing multiple roles, mistress and her attending servants. Hearing her, Kabir slowed down before reaching the door, keeping out of sight.

"It's my decision," he heard his wife say with impatient arrogance. "Who will dare tell *me* how to dress?"

"Yes, madam," Anwara responded in the voice of a servant.

"I'm beautiful, and I'm unashamed of my beauty."

"Yes, madam, yes. You are beautiful." Another mocking impression of a subservient attendant.

"Get out of here, everyone. Now!"

After watching her stare at herself in the mirror for a minute, Kabir said, "Are they all gone?"

"Yes," Anwara said, as though she had been aware of him the whole time. "But you need to ask permission before entering."

"Very well, madam," Kabir dropped to his knees, with a smile and hands clasped over his heart. "Begging the fair madam of the house for permission to enter her chamber."

"No." Anwara turned away from the mirror. She strolled toward the bed. "Permission denied."

"Why?"

"Rough, unruly men are not allowed inside here. This is a place of beauty."

"And what about those of us who love and appreciate beauty?"

"Does not make you beautiful." She sat daintily at the edge of the bed and crossed her legs.

Kabir spied no petticoat. Just her thin, strong ankles, the skin of her legs granite smooth and dark, and her legs, one dangling over the other, showing him just enough to keep him wondering. He liked the chipped nail polish on her toes, her worked-over feet with their scratchy skin, especially the hardened heels that tore track marks on his legs during sex and burned at the first touch of water like fire ants.

"I bathed today, madam," said Kabir.

"So? Clean doesn't mean beautiful."

"What makes you think you're the most beautiful woman in the world, madam?"

"Leave." Anwara pushed to her feet. "Leave. Right now."

"What have I done?" Kabir, still on his knees, playfully batted his eyes.

"Get out of here." Anwara gritted her teeth.

Her seriousness drew Kabir to his feet.

"No," said Kabir. "No more of this foolishness. Come downstairs. Put away everything where it belongs. Enough is enough."

Anwara walked toward her husband with unhurried steps, her swagger belying the urgency in her tone of admonishment. She stopped when she reached the space between bedroom and hallway, looked her husband in the face for as long as it took her to blink, and drew the door shut.

Falling asleep on the cane sofa for the second night in a row, Kabir wondered if these nights were the beginnings of a lifetime of quarreling.

Fitful sleep carried him through the early hours of the night. He had no idea what time it was when he gave up, swung his legs to the floor, and drew his heavy head off the cushion that might as well have been a wooden board. Moonlight was everywhere. Kabir craned his neck to look out the window at their room in the servants' quarters. Their abandoned bed prompted an image: of death having carted off someone that was neither him nor his wife but leaving their bed forever haunted.

At the entrance to the hallway that led to the bedroom, Kabir stopped. His ears pricked up at the suggestion of a sound that seemed to come from far away, possibly next door, or across the street, maybe even a few houses down in either direction, and yet its tonal clarity was as sharp as if it were playing on headphones pressed to his ears. Kabir's first thought was that it was Anwara. But as he listened, the direction of the sound became clear, as did its missive of distress. The stairs, and the sound, which he was sure by now was a low human moan, were to his left. He bounded down the stairs two steps at a time, slipping on the last step when he reached the first floor and falling on his knee. The pain stabbed through his kneecap, sending shockwaves up his thigh.

Ramzan's chair was vacant. Kabir rushed toward the back of the house, in the direction of the servants' quarters, and when he was near the garage and the bench where he sat and smoked his beedis, he called out the night guard's name. Hearing Kabir's voice, the moaning he had heard rose to a wail, a desperate cry for help.

"Over here," Ramzan called from behind the servants' latrine.

Getting closer, Kabir saw the beam of Ramzan's flashlight locked on the petrified, pain-stricken face of a young man, streaming with sweat or tears—it was hard to tell—seated and pushed up against the rear boundary wall of the house just a few feet from the latrine.

"Look at this," said Ramzan, shaking his head. "Boy wants to be a thief but he can't hold his water when he's caught."

"I beg you, let me go," the young man wept.

"Shut up. Stop crying." Ramzan raised a hand that threatened to crash down on the young man's face, making him wince and causing another wail. "I swear on my sons' lives, I'll call the police right now if you make one more sound."

"Oh mother! Oh God! I beg you, my father, I beg you, no police." He grabbed for Ramzan's legs, but stopped with a sudden scream. "Oh mother! Oh God! Oh mother!"

"This is what happens when boys try to act like men," said Ramzan. "Damn fool. What did you gain? Huh? Anything? Just made my night more stressful than I needed it to be."

"You caught him?" said Kabir.

"Didn't have to. Dumb bastard fell trying to be smart with the wire on the wall. Probably broke his leg."

"Oh mother! Oh God!" the young man carried on.

"So? What do we do with him?" said Kabir.

"If he could stand, I would have been happy to break both his legs myself. You hear me, boy?"

"Oh mother, I beg you, please help me."

"Help you?" Ramzan loomed over the young man, appearing larger than his diminutive size. "You want us to help you? Who told you to be a thief? You thought you were too smart for your own good? Now what will you do if we leave you here to die?"

"Oh my mother!" the young man wailed. "I beg you, have mercy, my father."

"Shut up. I'm not your father." Ramzan threatened him with the flashlight, its beam dancing madly in the darkness. "One more shout and you'll be handed over to the police. You hear me? Do you hear me? Nod your head. No sound."

Kabir watched in amazement Ramzan's skill at keeping the intruder in a state of panic as well as getting him to respond exactly the way he wished. The young man nodded.

"What's your name?" Ramzan asked. "Speak, boy, I give you permission."

"Litton," the young man whimpered.

"Where do you live? Oh, for God's sake, you're not dying. Be a man. A broken leg never killed anyone. Do as I say and tomorrow you'll have that leg set just right. Now, where do you live?"

"Over there." Litton waved a weak, perfunctory hand behind him.

"Over there where? Behind this boundary wall?" said Ramzan. "Boy, I'm an old man, and you've tested me tonight. Talk sensibly or you *will* die here."

"Oh my God! Oh my mother..."

"Here," Ramzan handed the flashlight to Kabir. "Hold it over him. I'll help him to his feet. We'll get him upstairs."

Litton sat awkwardly on Kabir and Anwara's bed, resting on an elbow while his other hand hovered over his injuries, both on the same leg, While his shin was torn and bleeding, it was clear that, at worst, the young man had a sprained ankle.

Ramzan stood back watching him like a jailer. A few paces behind him, Kabir wondered about the old night guard's next move, even as thoughts of his wife alone and asleep in the main house made him want to end this as quickly as possible.

"Do you know what would have happened to you if the master of this house was here tonight?" said Ramzan. "You'd be hanging by your balls from one of the trees out there. He's a powerful man with connections. You, boy, are a piece of filth for him. You get what I'm saying?"

Shaking and dumbstruck, Litton wiggled his head in agreement.

"You don't get a damn thing," said Ramzan. "What I'm telling you, you imbecile, is that this is the luckiest night of your sorry life as a thief. A lousy thief like you needs to take stock, find something else in life. Because next time, boy, I promise you, luck will kick you so hard that you won't know your head from your ass. Now do you understand what I'm saying?"

"God bless you, my father," Litton sputtered.

"Bless yourself," said Ramzan. "I'm not your bloody father."

"Look at him go," said Ramzan. "All that acting, and now he's off like a rabbit."

Ramzan had purposely drawn out his captivity, until Litton was too distraught to cry or be in fear and lapsed into a quiet state of confusion. It was at that point that the night guard offered him a glass of water, gave him a last warning to keep away from the neighborhood on future bumbling attempts at thieving, pulled him off the bed by his ear, and escorted him down the steps of the servants' quarters, all the way out the main gates. Once outside, and released, Litton dashed away, limping a run that made him look like he was on fire.

"Idiot," Ramzan grumbled.

"It's good that he didn't break that leg, or anything else," said Kabir. "What would we have done?"

"Who knows, young blood. Fools these days, can't even climb a wall properly."

"You wanted him to be able to get in properly and steal?"

Ramzan laughed. "That little idiot couldn't steal the coins from a blind man's cup without tripping over himself."

A soft light pooled around them. Kabir knew, as he was turning toward it, that it was glowing out of the bedroom window. His wife was awake.

"I'm going to go inside and make tea," said Ramzan. "It'll calm my heart."

"You did the right thing," said Kabir. "Letting that boy go."

"Maybe," Ramzan stopped on his way past Kabir to the kitchen. "If he tries again, he won't be so lucky. I've seen fools like him beaten to within inches of their lives for less. Whatever's written for him will happen."

Anwara was facing the window with the curtains parted just enough to be able to stare out. Kabir reached the bedroom and lightly tapped on the door with the tip of a finger.

"What was going on out there?" she asked, not turning from the window.

"The least competent thief in the city tried to climb over the boundary wall," Kabir said. "I had no idea Ramzan was such a hard nut."

"I did." Anwara closed the curtains. "There's more man in him than people see."

"Except *you* can see it clearly."

"Yes. And what did you do with the least competent thief in the city?" She stepped in front of the mirror.

"Nothing," said Kabir. "He fell and hurt himself. We let him go."

"Poor thing," Anwara smoothed the skin under her eyes. The sari from earlier had been replaced by a cream-colored house-dress. Sheathed in it, her complexion appeared a rich, dark chocolate brown, soft, lush, warm from sleep, and beckoning. "At least he should have been able to take something away."

"Like what?"

"Something. Some of the junk that's all over this house. It's not as if it would be missed."

"You're out of your mind," said Kabir. "The shrew would know before even setting foot inside the house. She'd smell it."

Anwara pivoted on a heel, slowly, lightly, and cocked her head to one side.

"What were you doing?" she said.

"When?"

"When Ramzan was taking care of the worst thief in Dhaka?"

Kabir recalled the scene in the servants' quarters, in their room, with the bleeding, trembling intruder on their bed, and Ramzan playing jailer. Kabir saw himself standing at the door holding the flashlight, doing nothing more than watching the night guard harass the thief. Doing nothing that contributed to the interrogation, that is. For there was nothing for him to do. There was no danger to be managed, and their intruder had done the job of disabling himself. What Kabir did do made him grin.

"Why the silly smile?" his wife asked.

"I did nothing," Kabir said.

"Doesn't surprise me."

"No?"

"No."

"You think your husband is *that* good for nothing?"

"No. You don't know how to be violent."

"There was no need for it. A child could have taken care of that fool."

"You are too gentle." Anwara held out her hand. "Come."

When they were in bed he said, "I was doing something."

"Yes?" Anwara's palm, flattened against Kabir's waist, slid down and up, causing small gasps to interrupt his speech.

"I was," he began, and Anwara's palm moved down and to the front of his thigh. "Thinking of you up here, asleep."

"I was sleeping very deeply. Too deep even for dreams to get in."

"You heard nothing?"

"No."

"I didn't either. Until I was up. I tried to sleep again on that damn thing outside. What the hell is it? It's not a sofa, it's not a bed. It's a large piece of wood with other pieces of wood on it."

"This is so much better, no?"

"Yes."

"You were thinking about me," Anwara said.

"The lady of the house, sleeping, comfortable, safe," Kabir muttered as they fell onto the bed.

By and by, tone-deaf tunes scaled up the walls of the house, leaking in through the windows and going entirely unnoticed.

The Father and the Judge

The father arrived before dawn. He accepted a glass of water from the servant boy and, after drinking all of it in one gulp, stood by the main gate, gazing wistfully at the ground. He was a middle-aged man in good health: tall and slender, white hair combed back, bristly white eyebrows over curious eyes, full lips the color of plums. His typed letter had come by post a week ago. Now the judge wished he could take back his response agreeing to see him.

He was from the village in Sylhet where the old Qureshi mansion still stood. For years, the landlord AR Qureshi had lived in the house and overseen the family lands, and the tenants who lived under his protection answered to him. Back then, it was common knowledge that all matters large or small, in spite of being under the jurisprudence of the erstwhile village council—presently the bureaucratic stranglehold known as the Zilla Parishad—ultimately required a Qureshi stamp. Now no Qureshis remained in the village. The house was locked up. The judge had paid the place a visit shortly after the landlord's death, found it dismal, and had no reason to want to return. His third cousin, Waseem Qureshi, had taken the mansion under his charge, along with a bungalow and small tea factory in Srimangal.

The servant boy brought tea and set it on the cane table. The judge asked if the man had said anything, asked for food or had been given any, but the boy shook his head.

He told the boy to fetch the letter from his office. The judge waved a hand at the father, realizing as the man began making his approach that he knew his name from his letter: Shamsher Ali. The man had signed it in Bangla.

He stopped a few feet from the edge of the steps that went up to the veranda and salaamed the judge, but did not make the customary attempt to touch the judge's feet in obeisance. The boy returned with the letter. The judge took a sip of tea, set down his cup, and lifted the letter. "How did you find my house?" he asked.

Shamsher Ali cleared his throat, which the judge found perfunctory. "In the village, people know your family better than their own households," he answered.

Without taking the letter out of the envelope, the judge referred to it. "All this is true?"

Shamsher Ali rolled his shoulders, let out a breath and peered at the judge from under his fierce brows. "What kind of father would make up such things about his daughter?"

The judge tapped the edge of the envelope on the back of his wrist. "I've read the letter. Now you need to tell me in your own words what happened, and what's still happening."

"All my own words, sahib, are in the letter," said Shamsher Ali.

"Why did you have it typed out in English and not write it by hand yourself? You sign your name well enough."

"My writing is too crude for a man of your level. I wanted it to look and sound right. I had it prepared professionally. Besides, everything official is done in English."

It must have cost him no small amount. And technically, the words were not purely his, but their transcribed, translated versions, generated by the typist. The judge sipped his tea and nodded.

"Waseem sahib has helped me and my family out many times," Shamsher Ali continued.

The judge wondered if it was his way of pitting one family member against another in a bid for supremacy of charity. "Then why not go to him?" he asked.

"I need the law, sahib. To protect my daughter." After a silence, he said, "The truth is, sahib, I did go to him. Waseem sahib, he told me to write to you."

The judge hid his surprise at this. A good ten years had passed since he had last seen his cousin. Their acquaintance, formed late in life, had always been distant, formal—not familial—because of the myriad circumstances spinning within family relations that can keep third cousins implicit strangers.

"Did you bring your daughter with you?"

Shamsher Ali's gaze dropped to the ground. His hands moved around to his back and gripped each other at the base of his spine. "She is safe," he said. "For now."

The story Shamsher Ali told the judge, speaking slowly and methodically—rather a bit too methodically, to the judge's chagrin—was that his daughter had been married three years to a man who had progressively degenerated into a tyrant. It wasn't always so, Shamsher Ali was quick to point out. As a prospective groom, he had showed plenty of promise, which, at the time the marriage was arranged, included a job lined up in the Middle East. The first year-and-a-half of marriage went as smoothly as could be expected. Shamela, the daughter—the alleged adulteress—had no complaints. But by the end of the second year, Shamela had had no children, and village gossip began spreading. A visit to a doctor in Sylhet proper proved it was not Shamela's inability to conceive. Before long, the gossip pegged the husband as being impotent. And so began his unwinding.

Shamela endured the beatings, shrugged off the bruised eyes and cut lips. Shamsher Ali was not one to interfere, but the girl's mother was unabashed in her probing of her daughter for details, deeming the gossip circulating over the girl's head a liability.

The judge held up a hand. "You've come all this way to tell me of village gossip? Sounds like you have your answer from the doctor. If that was indeed what was causing the problem."

Shamsher Ali said nothing, made no claims justifying his story, no refutations, and waited respectfully to be given permission to go on.

On a few occasions, Shamela was found unconscious and alone, her screams the night before not having drawn any of the neighbors, or her in-laws, to her rescue. Shamsher Ali approached the boy's father, and was shunned. The man accused Shamsher Ali of lying about his daughter, of dumping her onto his good and capable son, casting an evil eye over the boy's future and wanting to leech off of it, and now dragging his family's name through the mud.

City doctors be damned, the boy's father had roared, for no other reason than to make sure Shamsher Ali's humiliation reached as many ears as possible. His son was noble and pure and in perfect health, and it was his birthright to run his house the way he saw fit. No one less than the Almighty and His Prophet, peace be upon him, reserved rights of censure. Was it the boy's fault Shamsher Ali's loins had contributed to the world a defective girl? They should have drowned her at birth, saved themselves a lifetime's worth of trouble. And to top it off, she was a whore. No respectable whorehouse would employ a defective whore. On and on the boy's father berated him, until Shamsher Ali shrank from the heat of a thousand villagers' eyes burning into his skin.

The village elders were no better. They chastised Shamsher Ali for creating such a stir. For bringing shame on the village, disturbing its peace, and for meddling in other people's affairs. His daughter belonged to her husband and his family. She should be left to her fate. How did Shamsher Ali not know this?

The judge wanted to hear what that fate was. He wanted to hear it from Shamsher Ali.

Shamsher Ali's hands unclasped behind his back and pressed together at the level of his chest. "My child, sahib. I'm begging you for her life."

"Don't beg. I didn't agree to hear you beg. Certainly not for anyone's life."

Shamsher Ali's hands dropped to his sides.

"What about this business of adultery?" the judge asked.

"They are saying so, sahib."

"Based on what? Gossip? I don't have the patience to hear about gossip. I don't care what your village elders listen to. Gossip is trash and those old men should know better."

"On my child's soul, sahib, based on nothing but lies spread by her husband and his people."

"Where is your daughter now?"

"In a safe place, sahib."

For the second time the judge warily accepted this reply.

"Listen to me very closely," he said. "When you bring a petition to a court of law, the first thing you have to do is state everything, absolutely everything, clearly. No detail is too small. If you hold back, you only hurt your case. I've been doing this long enough to read people before they open their mouths. You're an honest man, I see that, but even the best of our intentions get clouded by emotion. It's human, it happens. I said I've read your letter more than once, and each time, I've been left wondering what is not in it. Why don't you tell me what the letter has left out?"

Shamsher Ali buried his face in his cupped palms. The backs of his hands were crisscrossed with scars, the fingers bony and robust, the yellowed nails jagged and cracked.

The judge sipped his tea. Later that day, as Chairman of the International Crimes Tribunals, he would listen as the chief prosecutor and other state investigative agencies brought charges against Mullah Khoda Baksh, a Jamaat-e-Islami hardliner who had allied himself with the Pakistan Army in 1971, and led them to the doorsteps of Bengalis to be rounded up and killed.

Shamsher Ali's hands slid off like a mask to reveal his face.

"She will not just be ruined, sahib. Her life is in danger."

"Ruined?"

"Her life, sahib." His hand brushed over his heart again.

The judge placed the letter on his lap and tapped a finger on it. "Why ruined?"

"My wife is still in the village. She is also in danger. But it's our home, and her people are nearby, too. Three generations, it's been our home. My forefathers, and me, we have eaten your salt."

"What about your people?"

Shamsher Ali shook his head. "No, sahib. They want nothing to do with this."

"So your wife is making sure your three-generation-old home doesn't disappear while you're here trying to save your daughter's life from ruination and death? And the girl is supposedly somewhere safe? If you were in my place, what would you think of your story?" The already-long day was growing even longer.

"Your family has been like God to us."

"Nonsense. How long do you plan on being here, keeping your daughter in her safe place?"

"Nobody will come near her if they know she has your family's protection."

The boy brought out the cordless phone. The judge took it, listened, nodded, and spoke once. He returned the phone to the boy when he was done. The boy slipped back into the house.

"I have to go now," he told Shamsher Ali. "In the meantime, think about what I've said." After a pause he said, "Come back in the evening."

At dinner, the judge wondered if his questioning of Shamsher Ali had been too severe. The judge's mind had latched onto the spotty tale of the village father fighting for his daughter's name, and, possibly, her life, even as his day at court was ruled by conspiracies, treason, death squads, and mass murder. Mullah Baksh had been barely prepared to say his name. Straight-backed, unmoving, unblinking, and calm, he looked like the wise leader of a wronged minority placed on trial by an oppressive government for fighting for his people's civil and human rights, while one after another of the reasons to hang him were announced.

Shamsher Ali had not left the house. The boy told the judge that he had asked only for water and refused food or tea. The judge brought his pipe to the veranda and once more summoned the petitioner.

"You've been here all day," said the judge. "Your daughter must be very safe where she is."

"She is, God willing." His soft voice was hoarse. His cheeks had shrunk, caved in, his full mouth thinned out and become a chapped and flaky gray.

"Have you thought about what I said in the morning?" the judge asked.

"I tried." Shamsher Ali's haggard appearance belied his resolve.

"You tried?"

"I did. I'm still not sure, sahib, what it is you wanted me to think about? My daughter faces mortal danger the moment she's seen back in the village."

"How long do you intend to stay in the city?"

"As long as it takes."

"And your wife? She's by herself in the village, isn't she?"

"She's safe, sahib."

"If your family is already so safe, why have you come here?"

"You are a man who lives his life seeking justice. That is what I'm seeking."

The judge emptied his pipe into an ashtray, suddenly exhausted. The tribunals were going to be long. His colleagues gave the impression of swiftness, all of them seeing blood before facts, down to Shamsuzzaman, who was known, even beyond the call of profession, for his unshakable grip on neutrality. Two of the scores of professors dragged out of their homes and shot in the middle of the night by Pakistani soldiers in December '71 were Shamsuzzaman's childhood friends. The judge had gotten the feeling at the end of this first day that patience among his colleagues in these proceedings would be at best a tenuous virtue.

"I have to be up early," said the judge.

"I will come back tomorrow."

Dr. CM Khan's stethoscope dangled like a trunk as he pumped the bladder that tightened the cuff around the judge's arm, then looked over the rim of his glasses at the reading.

"I never know what to make of that look," said the judge.

"Habit," Dr. Khan peeled the Velcro and undid the cuff. "Your blood pressure I can tell you from memory, as I can my own birthday. I don't remember the last time it was different. It's mine that will strike me down one of these days."

"Come have the bland food you've cajoled me into eating for years more often, share in my misery, let our blood pressures commiserate."

"You don't need mine corrupting yours. And without salt I would give up food altogether, which I will not do. Moderation is a weakness, and doctors make the worst patients. So we make our destinies."

The judge rolled down his shirtsleeve and buttoned it at the wrist. Dr. Khan's stethoscope banged against the edge of his desk as he took his seat.

"Stay with the regular vitamins," he said, "and it's not too late to get a bad habit to give things a stir."

"I still smoke my pipe."

"Might as well drink milk after dinner and call it living dangerously. So, what seems to be the trouble that you look like the condemned man and not the judge?" He began scribbling wide looped letters and curlicues on his prescription pad. "I know you're forbidden to talk about you-know-what, but I wouldn't want you to—even if you were dying to pour your heart out about it. There are better ways of making oneself sick. Who gives a good goddamn what happens to those old goats at this point? Even they don't. Let them be. They'll die eventually." He tore off the sheet and slid it on top of a small stack under a glass paperweight.

"There's a man, from the village, who's come to see me," said the judge. "Some trouble with his family."

Dr. Khan rose from his chair, chuckling, and his stethoscope banged once more against the desk before settling over his belly. "And you find yourself tied to traditional obligations," he said, as though completing the judge's thought.

"Damn shame," Dr. Khan's tongue clucked. "Long ago, I told any damn fool thinking they could come to hang themselves at my door to die first before making the trip. It's my wife's damn sentimentality that has these people taking advantage of her."

The judge's head nodded. He fixed his tie, smoothed the front of his shirt, and slid his arms through the sleeves of his suit jacket, then checked the inside pocket for his pipe.

"I can't just turn him away, if what he's saying is true," he said.

"Is he seeking money or rights over some godforsaken old property? Which you people have had in loads no doubt."

"Nothing like that." The judge felt for his matches in his breast pocket.

"Then send him off to his village and remind him to forget his way back to your door."

The judge enjoyed the doctor's turns of phrase. A few pegs of Scotch later, which were still hours away from happening at the Dhaka Club, his poetics would wax until the last of his drinking mates bid him goodnight.

"But don't listen to my damn foolish notions." Dr. Khan clapped the judge's back, a little too hard as always, and turned the judge's shoulder toward the door. Maybe the doctor had planned an earlier start today on the Scotch. "See you next month."

Shamsher Ali, wearing the same clothes as the day before, stood before the judge once more. The judge had read the letter again the night before, trying to look past the mechanical staccato of the transcription, imagining them being spoken by Shamsher Ali. How had the man relayed them to the typist? What had the typist heard? Did the typist pause at places to regard the dictation he was taking? Did he ask questions? Had he taken down every word verbatim? Or as close to verbatim as he could, molding them from Bangla into English? Had he censored anything? How scrupulous had his judgment been?

A detailed enumeration of the crimes of Mullah Khoda Baksh would be presented today. Meetings he had hosted with Pakistani army officers and Jamaat-e-Islami partisans where plans to target Bengali intellectuals were hatched. Al-Badr, Al-Shams paramilitary death squads sanctioned by Pakistani generals with Baksh at the helm, organizing, recruiting, deploying.

If it were a truly international tribunal, the generals would be the ones on the stand, subpoenaed out of retirement and denial, and placed under the spotlight. Pictures of them listening to the actuality of their crimes from witnesses and survivors, akin to the one of Adolf Eichmann in headphones, on trial, trapped in his glass cage, would be blazed across the world media. Yahya, Tikka, Farman, Niazi—every bit as monstrous as Hitler's executioners.

Shamsher Ali was disheveled, giving off the ripe odor of unwashed clothes and skin.

"How is your daughter doing?" The judge tried taking a sip of tea.

"Safe for now," Shamsher Ali said feebly.

The judge set his cup down. "Eventually you and daughter will have to go back. Resume your lives. No matter what. Am I wrong?"

Shamsher Ali drew a long breath. "How it will be possible only God knows."

"It will be possible," said the judge.

"Yes, with your family name and blessing, no one will dare raise a finger against us."

"So. This comes down to my throwing around my family name on your word. And then what? Every time there's a village matter there will be a line outside my gate."

"Your family, sahib—"

"Stop telling me about my family," the judge's knee pushed against the cane table as he leaned forward, sloshing tea over the rim of the cup. "Where is your daughter? I want to know from her mouth, hear her tell me all the things you've said. I'm not one of your blind village elders. Things don't work like that here. Bring your daughter here. I want to hear what she has to say."

"On her soul, I give you my word, sahib." His hands were trembling as he clasped them together in front of him to keep control.

"You don't want her to speak for herself?"

"She is afraid, sahib."

"You said she's safe. She will be safe here in my house. No one knows you in this city, no one knows her, except for the people you've entrusted with her safekeeping. Right? So, bring her here. Let her speak for herself. Let me hear her."

Shamsher Ali's hands broke free of each other. The judge was on the verge of dismissing him for good, sending him on his way to whatever fate awaited him.

In all his years on the bench, the judge had sent one man to the gallows. Three days after the man's neck broke, new evidence surfaced that could have reduced his sentence to life in prison. The judge had been a lifelong proponent of the death penalty, but that case had been damning. The soul Shamsher Ali spoke of, if such a thing existed in men and women, whether it flowed in his veins, lived embedded in his flesh, wherever in whatever form it was supposed to exist unseen had since that midnight fifteen years ago been shaken.

A brief conference with Shamsuzzaman at the end of yesterday had left no doubt in the judge's mind where his colleagues already stood. Baksh would hang.

"Bring her here," said the judge. "You're a reasonable man and a father protecting his daughter. I don't have children, but it doesn't take much of a stretch of imagination to understand that much."

Shamsher Ali's eyes wandered, cast around, his hopes seeking a place to moor.

"Have something to eat before you go," the judge said, pushing himself to his feet.

"Sahib." Shamsher Ali took a step forward. "I beg your forgiveness. What you told me to think about, I did think about. You want to hear everything from my daughter's mouth, and so I will bring her here and throw her at your feet. She has ruined my reputation in the village. I should leave her to her fate. I should. Everything we could manage we gave for her dowry. And what does she go and do? Turn her ungrateful, disloyal back on us."

"What do you think you should have done?" the judge asked.

"It pains me to think it."

"I should throw you out of my house."

"I will drag her here by her ears."

"I'm not interested in your family drama. You come here, to my house, wanting justice, and you don't pay me the courtesy of being straightforward from the outset."

"What do you want to know about me, sahib? I will stay here day and night until I have earned your trust."

"And your daughter is so well guarded and safe wherever she is that there's no limit on the time she can stay there," the judge pressed on, reluctantly.

"She is not, sahib. God will know the truth, no matter how I wish to evade it. I don't know where she is. She has run away."

"You have real problems," said the judge. "Problems far out of my reach. Have you filed a police report? What about the Zilla Parishad?"

"I'm a poor farmer, sahib. Son and grandson and great-grandson of servants and farmers. The police and Zilla Parishad see me as they see insects. As a nuisance. I don't have money to appear before them. Without money, they have no ears for people like me."

The judge moved to the edge of the steps, towering over Shamsher Ali even though he was a head shorter than him. From a distance Shamsher Ali's face gave off the sheen of health and vitality, but up close it was a sun-scorched leathery tan. Lines ran along his forehead like they were cut straight across with a scalpel. Crow's feet wrinkled the corners of his eyes.

"How much value does your own word have for you?" the judge asked.

Shamsher Ali's eyes narrowed, pinching the crow's feet, as if a sudden light had flashed in his pupils. "It is my word, sahib. All that I have in the world."

"Then you will appreciate the value my word has to me. Which you want me to put on the line for you."

A phone call to the Sylhet District Bar Association and to Ansar Wahab, his old law firm partner and classmate from Dhaka University, was how far the judge's word would have to reach and be put to the test. But it would not be much of a test. Ansar loved nothing more than a tussle with the village elders and Zilla Parishad types. Throw in greedy policemen waiting for their palms to be greased, and pro bono would be a small price for Ansar to endure for the sheer pleasure of the fight. The judge's word would not be at risk. Ansar would make it a personal matter, and the use of his official credentials would go no further than as a glorified ID badge.

The boy appeared holding the cordless phone in front of him like a sacred offering. The judge took it and checked his watch. There was plenty of time before the day's session would be called to order.

Shamsuzzaman's voice piped over the line, eager, frenetic, like he'd just sprinted half a mile to make the call. There was a situation. Protestors for the Jamaat-e-Islami opposition, outside the courthouse, were demanding the immediate release of Mullah Baksh, as well as the suspension of "these satanic trials by infidels and traitors and conspirers with Hindus." It was no small crowd, and it was swelling by the second. Some lawyers had been attacked, stoned. Shamsuzzaman declared he was ready to give his verdict. "Let's put the bastard's neck in the noose." Mir Ahsan Latif was also resolved, as were the chief prosecutor and investigative committees, to send Mullah Khoda Baksh's life marching toward its (just and long-awaited) end.

He had been silent long enough for Shamsuzzaman to wonder. The judge blinked out of his reverie and, as a sign of acknowledgment, cleared his throat. The proceedings would start on schedule, Shamsuzzaman said. "No Jamaat bastards are going to prevent the law from functioning, let me tell you, let them burn down the city if they will. Every drop of blood and every bone in that murderer's body will answer for his crimes."

After hanging up, the judge met Shamsher Ali's stare. The judge had no doubt that the man would stand there for as long as it took.

"Go back home," the judge said, softly.

"Every word I've told you is true, sahib."

"I know. But I still don't understand why you didn't tell me. It's not the way to gain the trust of—when you have nothing to hide."

"It was my shame, sahib," said Shamsher Ali. "That's what I was hiding."

"In a court of law it would only weaken your case." The judge said this and wanted to take it back the next moment. "Pride is the worst thing to bring to your defense."

"Take good care of her." The judge weighed his next words before speaking them. "Don't keep her married to that man. That's all I have to say. Anything else you do is your business."

Shamsher Ali nodded, his eyes blinking.

The judge dialed the operator and waited to be connected to Ansar, imagining the glee behind his grumbling façade at the thought of shaking down village bureaucrats and the girl's in-laws, and wondering, too, what his old law firm partner would have to say about the tribunals.

A lot, no doubt. A lot.

Dual Income

Maruf was against Salma returning to work, but not because he thought she was incapable. He was, simply put, old-fashioned. Salma had been fine with being a housewife. Fifteen years had passed since she had last taught: a decade and a half during which they had two children, a military government came to an end, religious fanatics returned to the frontlines of Bangladeshi politics, democracy got tossed around like a piece of hot coal no one could handle, and Maruf's prospects of a major promotion after ten years in the same non-management position turned into a pay cut.

"Mergers," said Maruf, "it's code word for murder, because that's what it does to real working people. Bleeds them dry in broad daylight. Americans love mergers more than they love their families."

Maruf's bank had been taken over by an American investment firm. Over the last six weeks, representatives had been arriving every other day—clean-cut, smiling faces torched and ruddy from the Dhaka heat but maintaining youthful grace. They spent interminable hours behind the locked door of the conference room with the chairman and CEO Mr. Moazzem, who also faced the unenviable prospect of becoming a menial employee. Mr. Moazzem had asked Maruf if there was anything he could do to help. He actually meant it. After a few days' thought, and a serious conversation with Salma that caused them to bicker, Maruf begrudgingly asked Mr. Moazzem to recommend his wife to a good firm.

"It's not what I want, sir, but times are—"

"I understand, Maruf."

Mr. Moazzem delivered. One of the top industrialists in the city had opened a new office, and administrative positions were open but filling fast.

As soon as Salma excitedly mentioned her CV, Maruf said that it needed to be updated, no matter that she hadn't had a job since she was in school. For a firm of this caliber it would have to be close to perfect and make up in appearance what it was lacking in substance. A proper cover letter also needed to be drafted. She would need a quick course on basic computer use, emailing, searching the web, none of which, Maruf grumbled, could be added to her skill set.

"That part will have to remain un-updated," Maruf puffed out his cheeks and exhaled. "We could possibly fatten the administrative background from your teaching days with emphasis on organization, timeliness, account-ability—" the words swam into each other in Salma's ears "—even if most of these positions are little more than office- boy-type work, with all due respect to Mr. Moazzem. At least the firm has a name and reputation."

He went through a checklist as if evaluating his own prospects for the job. He stopped and asked her if she was really prepared to go through the headache of all this. The headache, she told him, seemed only to be his. She was fine. They needed this to work. Maruf's pride thus dented, he resumed his advice.

The city was different from when Salma was last part of it on a daily basis. There were more cars, more buses, more trucks, more damned rickshaws and scooters, more people, more accidents. Once a week at least Maruf saw a deadly crash or a bus hitting a scooter or rickshaw and killing a family. Then there were the student thugs and religious fundamentalists who needed absolutely no reason to unleash violence on whoever they decided was the day's target, there were the young cretins who had no respect for women and touched and groped and tried to rip their clothes off out in the open. Dhaka was not what it used to be.

There was a time, Maruf elaborated with a eulogizing sadness, when children and women could walk freely, unmolested on any street at any time; when men were protectors, husbands, fathers, and respectful heads of households, not miscreants ganging up with others in the name of religion and solidarity and politics and righteousness to turn the city into a jungle. At the end of his ruminations, he said, without making eye contact with her, "There's time still to think about it. These things happen in every job. I know people who have gone through worse. Some are doing even better than before."

"I'm happy for those people." Salma was on her feet before Maruf could start up again, knowing well enough that the next installment of his tirade would feature the shameless leasing out of the country to the West.

She retrieved her old CV from the depths of a trunk that had been stowed away in the storeroom since they'd moved into the flat five years ago. She drew out the file like a fragile relic. Except for the dust and the mothball smell it was fine, no different than the day she'd wrapped it in the plastic bag and put it under a stack of books from her teaching days. She locked up the trunk, brought the file to the dining table, and untied the string that held it shut.

She could hear Maruf talking in the bedroom while he changed his clothes. Adil's footsteps banged around the veranda in the back. Shama's Bollywood music leaked out of her room and around the flat like a chorus of mosquitoes. The cook came out and asked Salma if he should set the table for dinner, and Salma gave him an absent-minded nod.

"No one has faith in the country anymore," Maruf was saying as he walked in. "Why wonder when outsiders and foreigners think it's theirs for the taking?" He came to the table and took the CV from Salma's hands. Holding it at arm's length, he started laughing. Salma snatched it back and tucked it into the file.

"Item one," he snorted, "bringing that thing from the Stone Age to the twenty-first century."

"Dipu downstairs is good with computers," said Salma. "He is a smart boy. He can do it."

"Are you mad? Letting a child do the work of a professional? Seriously, Salma, how do you come up with these foolish ideas?"

The cook began setting the table and bringing out dishes of food.

"For a job in a firm like this, you cannot be careless," Maruf said. "Everything has to be spotless and perfect. Believe me. Things are not what they used to be. All that flimsy, cobble-together-what-you-can attitude is history. Now the firms have trained people they hire just to look for mistakes and discrepancies in everything. Including cover letters and CVs."

Salma put the file down on the chair next to her. Maruf walked over and picked it up.

"My god," he chuckled, "I don't think they even make files like these anymore."

He smacked the file against his palm. "There is no point messing around," he said. "If we're going to do something, it should be done right. I will take this with me and have Pranab prepare the new ones. It will be a few days, things are very busy at the bank, but at least it will be done properly and responsibly."

Maruf spoke on, circling the dining table, hands clasped behind him. He put inflections in his speech on points he thought needed more stress, or else his wife would not fathom their seriousness. He stopped at the head chair at the opposite end of the table from her, leaned on it with both hands, and said, "No 'I beg to apply for the position' nonsense from the times of our fathers. Only direct, professional courtesy, and confidence in the applicant's potential as the best candidate for the job."

Salma saw the deep circles under his eyes, the doubts buried under the seemingly confident stare, the rasp in his breathing that had gotten worse, instead of better, because she knew he was still smoking.

"I will leave it to you," she said. "Whatever you think needs to be done."

Then she called for the children to come in for dinner.

Late that night, Maruf nudged Salma in bed. She had been trying to sleep for the last hour, but could do nothing more than count the things she would need to arrange and rearrange if she got hired. "What are you doing awake?" she asked him.

"I was thinking."

"Okay."

"You can really make something of this position if you do it right." Salma kept her back turned away from him as he continued: "It's a new branch of a major firm with international presence, and you're coming in at a good time, at the beginning."

"That's good." Sleep suddenly hit Salma. Her eyes grew heavy.

Maruf was silent for several minutes, and Salma drifted off.

"But don't overwork yourself," he said, jolting her awake. "You know? If they make you stay late, tell them you have a family. If they insist on overtime, then they will have to pay for it. You know? But it's best not to get ahead of ourselves. Nothing has happened yet. You know?"

"Hmm."

He shifted his position again, onto his back.

"Bastards," he murmured. "Bastards."

Three days later Maruf brought home the newly made cover letter and CV. He made a ceremony of sitting down in the living room, calling the children out, having Salma sit formally across from him, then presenting the documents to her, which were paper-clipped and encased in a smooth, clear plastic folder. He gave them a light tap with his palm for good measure.

"Well?" said Maruf. "Are you going to look or what? Even the paper is of good quality, used specially for official documents," he pointed out. "See for yourself," he said, as if she had challenged him.

"Where are the originals?" was the first thing Salma could think to ask.

"What originals?" Maruf frowned. "Those old things were useless. Open it, take a look."

The folder was heated from the sun. It leaked its warmth onto Salma's lap. Salma popped the clasp, reached in, and slid out the new documents. They made her sad, reminding her of the time her late father had had the old ones made.

"What do you think? Huge difference, no?" Maruf sat back smiling, triumph back in his bearing.

Salma gave a cursory nod and replaced the documents inside the cover with care as if they belonged to someone else.

"What is it for?" Shama asked.

"Yes, what is it for?" Adil repeated after his sister.

"Nothing for you two to worry about," Salma replied, placing the documents in their plastic folder on the coffee table.

"Go inside," said Maruf, standing. "Don't make me repeat myself."

Adil tore away from the chair before his father could speak again, tugging Shama by the sleeve of her kameez.

"What's the matter now?" Maruf asked.

"What did you do with the old papers?"

"Seriously, Salma? All the trouble I go to and you're worried about some old documents that were lying god-knows-where until a few days ago? I don't understand you."

"Trouble? You took them to the bank and someone else made a new set, and you brought them home."

"Unbelievable!"

"My father had them made."

Maruf exhaled noisily.

"Some days I don't know what gets into people in this house." He sat back down, stretched, and began untying his shoelaces. He pulled off one shoe and tossed it to the side, paused as if to consider a new strategy with the other, then sent that one the same way. The socks he peeled off like they were damaged skin that had to be carefully removed.

"Did you throw them out?" Salma asked.

"Throw what out?"

"Maruf, you know what."

"I don't know. I gave them to Pranab, he needed them to work from to make those," he pointed at the new documents. "I don't know what he did with them. Are you having second thoughts now?"

"No."

"Because if you are not one hundred percent sure you want to apply for this position, tell me. There is no turning back once you do. Not with a firm like this. Anyway, you should get those sent off immediately. They'll have a line of people begging for a job any given day. Unless you want me to take care of it?"

"No," Salma picked up the plastic folder again. "No."

She sent the cover letter and CV, two weeks went by, and Salma had as good as forgotten about it. Maruf mentioned it offhandedly, grumbled he wasn't really surprised, given Salma's lack of experience, and for a time the matter was put to rest. When the phone call came, Salma wasn't there to answer it because she was downstairs on the first floor haggling with the chicken seller. Shama had taken the call, and shouted for her mother down the stairwell.

A crisp, young female voice verified Salma's identity in English.

"Yes, I am Salma Karim."

"Are you able to come for an interview next Tuesday? Ten o'clock, sharp." She added the "sharp" as if she knew Salma to be compulsively tardy.

"Depending, of course, on things being peaceful in the city," she added.

"Yes."

"Good. My name is Anika. Just ask for me at reception. And if anything should change between now and then, we have each other's contact information."

Salma set down the receiver. Her heart was pounding, and she felt stricken with worry.

"That woman was rude," said Shama. "Are you going to work for her?"

Salma cupped Shama's chin. "I don't know. Maybe. Adil? Come out here."

With the two children, Shama went downstairs and knocked on Mrs. Mahbub's door.

"Who is it?" Mrs. Mahbub's voice floated from the back of the flat.

"Mrs. Mahbub, it's Salma, from upstairs."

There was silence, followed by approaching footfalls. Adil recoiled behind his mother, and Shama stood at Salma's side. The door opened. Mrs. Mahbub popped her head out. Her hair was gleaming with oil, and pulled tightly back, giving her an expression of perpetual shock. Pockmarks covered her cheeks. Over the thin line of her mouth was a fuzz of hair. She smelled of sandalwood and laundry soap.

Mr. Mahbub had left two years earlier for the daughter of an associate from work to whom he was now married. His conciliatory gestures were to buy his son an iMac with a 27-inch monitor, and a printer and scanner unit, and transfer ownership of the flat to Mrs. Mahbub—whom he never legally divorced—while he kept making the payments on it. Mrs. Mahbub did not file for divorce and believed that Dipu's father would eventually return.

"Mrs. Mahbub, I wanted to ask you something. Is this a good time?" said Salma.

"Oh, yes, yes! Come inside first. Hello children. Shama, you're going to be taller than your mother next time I see you. Dipu? Turn off that computer and come say hello to Salma auntie and the children. All day he is glued to that thing."

The dreary living room, the entire flat, was depressing. The shut windows and drawn curtains, the complete lack of natural light, gave the place a crypt-like chill. It was cold, too, almost frigid, as though the air conditioning had been running round the clock full blast. Most of the furniture was in need of repair, if not replacement. The sofa that Mrs. Mahbub gestured for them to take had holes in it, small ones, but large enough for puffs of bright white cotton to peek out. On a table next to the sofa was a framed picture of Dipu in his school uniform, holding up a certificate, the corners of his mouth drooped, his eyes half closed. Mrs. Mahbub flipped a switch, and the sudden glare of the uncovered overhead light bulb laid bare the drab gloom of the room.

Dipu, still in his school uniform, ambled into the room. He was pink-cheeked and fat. The hair on his head was like fine porcupine quills. His knees knocked, and he dragged his feet when he walked. Like his mother he wore thick glasses, behind which his eyes were two tiny dots. Without regarding the guests, he went to his mother's side, and stood looking at the ground.

"What do you say, Dipu?" said Mrs. Mahbub.

"*Hello*, Auntie," Dipu croaked.

"How are you, Dipu? How is school?" Salma asked.

Dipu didn't answer. Mrs. Mahbub offered to make tea, but Salma asked her not to go to the trouble.

"Do you children want Coke?" Mrs. Mahbub asked.

"Coke, yes!" Adil shouted.

"No. And be quiet." Salma clasped and tightened her arm around him. Shama said she didn't want anything.

"I might be getting a job, Mrs. Mahbub," said Salma.

"Things are bad at the bank with your husband?" Mrs. Mahbub asked.

"A little extra income would be good, yes," said Salma.

"When times get bad, they get bad."

"I know you know, Mrs. Mahbub." Salma felt awkward after making the comment.

"Do I know!" Mrs. Mahbub sighed. She swept a hand through Dipu's hair, which he dodged. "Every day I know." Dipu gave his mother a sideward frown, which she did not see.

"I only have the interview," said Salma. "God willing, if I get the position, will it be all right if the children stopped by here after school?"

"Yes, yes, of course, you don't need to ask even."

"Thank you. Dipu? Is it okay with you?" Salma asked.

"Dipu? What do you say?" Mrs. Mahbub touched her son's plump cheek. Dipu flinched and pulled away. "It will be nice for him. All the time he's home, he's on that thing," she waved in the direction of Dipu's room, indicating the computer.

"Also, if I get this job, I will need to know about computers. Dipu, would you like to be my teacher?" said Salma.

Dipu smiled. Two dimples dented his cheeks. "Okay."

After a short silence Salma thanked Mrs. Mahbub and promised to keep her updated. Mrs. Mahbub offered tea and refreshments again just as Salma had got to her feet, which made her feel embarrassed and opportunistic. She promised to stay for longer next time. Mrs. Mahbub saw them out and locked the door, and then they heard her call Dipu's name and her voice fading toward the back of the flat.

"That place makes me feel strange. It's such a sad home. No home should be sad like that," said Shama, bounding up the steps two at a time. Adil sprinted up behind her, slipped, knocked his knee on a step, and howled. Salma picked him up by an arm, and he dug his face into her shoulder. She couldn't help agreeing with her daughter.

Maruf sat on the edge of their bed staring at a vague point in front of him for several minutes. "Well, it's just an interview, probably one of several. Times are different. These days, firms like this especially go through many rounds before deciding."

"I thought you would be pleased," said Salma. "My interview is Tuesday."

Maruf craned his neck around like he was doing an after-workout stretch. "Pleased? About what? They probably have a hundred interviews lined up for just that one position."

"Even for jobs that are no better than an office boy's?" said Salma. Maruf made to reply but stopped.

"Tuesday, huh?" he said. "And that crazy woman downstairs, you want the children to stay with her?"

"She is not crazy, Maruf. Don't say that."

"Why else would her husband run off? And that poor boy, with nowhere to go and stuck with her day and night."

"Shama and Adil will not stay with her. They will only let her know when they come home. Just so someone knows. Cook will be busier with me gone and may not always be home."

"Hmm, well," Maruf began changing out of his work clothes. In his undershirt he looked small and defeated, like he had just been badly beaten and humiliated by an opponent, lost everything, and was hanging up his armor for good. "I'm glad they found the documents acceptable," he grumbled.

He didn't want dinner. Salma and the children ate in silence. Afterward Salma spoke to the cook for a few minutes, telling him that there was a chance she was going to be gone during the day starting soon.

In the bedroom she found Maruf staring at himself in the mirror attached to the adjoining bathroom door. Seeing her, he quickly grabbed his shirt, and threw it over his head.

"Are you worried about your figure?" Salma chided. "Is that why you didn't want to eat?"

"No," Maruf said curtly and picked up the folded newspaper on the ground next to the bed.

"It's good to be a little conscious," he said, after shuffling through the paper for a few minutes. "These young Americans that have been coming to the bank, you should see them. Their bodies and their health, and the women look stronger than the men. No wonder they, that whole country, are devouring the world in every way. Who can go against them when they're that well-fed and well-built?"

Salma got into bed as Maruf kept reading, or rather flicking from page to page, until she couldn't help being irritated by it.

"There is every chance that they won't like me," she said, without turning to face him. "Is that what you want?"

She heard him fold the paper meticulously and toss it on the floor.

"What nonsense are you talking?" he said. He slid down under the covers, gave them a pull to release them from the mattress at the foot of the bed and drew them up to his ears. Salma raised her head just as he was turning over.

"They sound like a place that I won't be qualified for," she said. "Even for a job no more than an office boy's. There are other places I can look."

"It's too late now. You have an appointment, and they're expecting you. My name is on the line. Last thing I need on top of everything else is my wife making me look like an idiot."

"Then you should have thought of that before." Salma looked at the bald patch at the top of his head, the hair around it sprouting like grass on the edges of a poorly maintained lawn. He moaned as he dozed off, gave a short grunt, and began snoring.

The morning of the interview was warm, with a brisk wind rising and falling every few seconds, carrying hints of the rain to come in less than a month. The sky was a dull slate gray. Maruf flagged two scooters, one for him and the children and one for Salma, but Adil wanted to go with his mother. Maruf ordered Shama to hold on to her brother, and wait in the other one. He then peeked his head into Salma's scooter.

"Keep this," he brought out a hundred-taka note. "Do you want me to go with you?"

"No. Just get the children to school."

"Listen. It is what it is. Don't try to show yourself off as something you're not." He waited, and then said, "Okay?"

"Okay."

"Here, keep my mobile, too. Just in case." Before she could respond Maruf placed the phone on her lap. He gave her another fifty-taka note, and flooded the scooter driver with the directions to where she was going so he could not charge a higher fare by taking a longer route.

Mrs. Mahbub and Dipu came out of the building. Mrs. Mahbub was talking to her son and, seeing her upstairs neighbors pulling away in the scooters, waved enthusiastically. Dipu was rushing toward a rickshaw he was trying to flag down at the same time.

On Shama's lap Adil was sniffling against his will. Maruf squeezed in next to them and addressed their driver in the same harsh tone as the other. Shama caught a glimpse of Dipu as the scooter engine revved under her seat, miserable and numb to his mother, scrambling onto the rickshaw as soon as it pulled up while Mrs. Mahbub talked on.

The office was on Motijheel Road. Despite the driver's age and innocuous appearance, Salma was skeptical that he would follow Maruf's instructions, but it became evident soon that in line with Maruf's orders he had taken Maulana Bhashani Road to get to the Motijheel area via Shahbag. The driver's trepidation, however, became evident as soon as they entered the Shahbag area. He slowed the scooter, pulled to the side of the road, and turned to Salma.

"Lady, I cannot go the way your husband told me to anymore," the driver said. He was in his seventies. His eyes were watery and looked blinded with cataracts. The cloth cap on his head was tilted to one side like someone had smacked it out of place. The grimace on his face gave Salma the fear that the he had suddenly become ill.

"Why not?" she asked.

The driver pointed ahead. Salma leaned to one side to look past him through the windshield. She could see nothing more than the usual—clots of people, buses, rickshaws, scooters, more people. Thinking she was missing something Salma kept looking, and the scooter driver, like a tutor who was waiting for the pupil to catch on to the obvious, sat fidgeting. Then Salma heard the chanting. It was concerted, unified, loud, and within moments the natural assembly of people and vehicles on the busy intersection grew into a dark wall of bodies. The scooter driver turned to Salma. When he opened his mouth to speak Salma saw that his teeth were destroyed by paan and betel nut.

"Please, there is no way to keep going," he said. "Forgive me. I won't take your money, but I cannot risk it. Even if I wanted to I couldn't. I will take you back to your home."

"Is there another way to go?" Salma asked.

The driver's anguish deepened. He lowered his head, and brought it up again.

"I cannot, Madam. Forgive me."

Salma wondered why Maruf had failed to mention a possible demonstration. If anything, it would be the first thing he would highlight above all else, above even the interview, before going on to lambaste the government and work himself into a sweat before huffing off petulantly as if it were all Salma's fault.

The sound of his complaints droned in her head. A stone grew in her stomach, heavy, oppressive, like it did not want her to stand on her feet again, would not allow it. Salma sat quietly with her eyes closed. The chanting from the demonstration grew louder. When she opened her eyes she noticed flags, their green as rich as rain-fed grass, and the circle in the center of the green as red as blood. They were flying on bamboo poles, large and small, waving and fluttering.

"I beg you, lady, let's turn around."

"No, I will get out here." Salma handed the driver the fifty-taka note and climbed out, the scooter immediately melting into the traffic behind her. She draped the strap of her handbag diagonally across her body and headed toward the demonstration. Soon she was trotting, as if rushing to catch a departing bus, her heart hammering in her chest. Her lungs started to burn, but within minutes her head felt light and detached from the rest of her body. She couldn't tell if the mass of bodies was moving toward her or away, and she didn't care. She was being propelled toward the crowd, for what reason she didn't know, but for the fact that even if she tried to stop and turn she would be unable to. She was near enough to see individual faces now. Faces painted in the colors of the flag. Faces pulled and stretched with fervor that Salma envied. Young faces, down to boys and girls no older than Shama and Adil, with banners raised, flags aloft, and chanting. Calling for the punishment of war criminals from the Liberation War with Pakistan.

Salma eased her pace and moved along the side of the road. The crush of bodies looked like it wouldn't allow a single inch for her to pass through. The demonstration was not moving forward, nor moving at all, as rigid and solid as a wall. They were shouting for justice, calling for death. Happily, jovially, they were demanding heads in nooses. Salma saw the name of the man currently on trial scrawled in Bangla across a banner that was bobbing up and down in the center of the crowd, his face, next to his name, circled within a noose. She saw a small opening between a few bodies, and plunged forward, bumping against a young woman on one side, and grazing the bare arm of a middle-aged man on the other. A girl, three or four, hovered above her, sitting on the shoulders of a man clutching a flag on a stick. An old couple held up the black- and-white portrait of a young man, most likely a son, murdered by the Pakistan Army.

A terrific din arose from the very heart of the procession. The young woman Salma had bumped into turned and gave her a big smile, and shouted a word of solidarity, pulling Salma into the spirit of the demonstration. Salma's heart thumped wildly but she felt calm, unthreatened in the midst of the crowd.

Riot police trickled out from places Salma couldn't see. Helmets, batons, shields, vests, guns. Their boots crunched, and, like the demonstrators, they moved to their own unified rhythm. The demonstrators didn't oppose the presence of the police, and neither were the police making threatening gestures at the crowd.

A great surge swept through the crowd, pushing it forward, and Salma felt its energy against her back as she went forward with it. She pressed her handbag to her side, feeling the bulge of Maruf's phone. In seconds the demonstration moved ten feet. The police seemed unperturbed, even calm. Salma felt the hand of the young woman beside her take hers and thrust it upward, like Salma had just won a boxing match. The woman shrieked so loudly that her words became incoherent, her voice a sloshing clot of phlegm and grit in her throat.

A huge response rang out of the crowd. Salma, certain now that she would miss the interview and that it didn't matter, gripped the young woman's hand and filled her lungs with air to shout.

The Caretaker's Dilemma

For Abdul Hamid being caretaker was easy. Having the worries of a father of a young, marriage-age daughter at his age was not. At seventy, with a bad heart and hypertension that was weakening his kidneys, Hamid counted every day as his last, with his main concern being to see his daughter married, even if he didn't live to see her children. Thirty-five years he'd been in the service of Harun Qureshi, taking care of the man's house with a distant devotion that seemed only to deepen with time. Now, in his old age, Hamid was faced with the greatest of all duties—finding a boy and being able to offer a suitable dowry.

Suitable, needless to say, being defined and determined by the boy's family. The exorbitant, ridiculous dowries a groom's family could demand were terrifying. There were countless horror stories of weddings canceled because the groom's family had decided to add a car or a house to the package at the last moment. When their abrupt demands could not be satisfied, they walked out. The shame was always the burden of the girl's side. It was the father who would be blamed, scorned for incompetence, charged with marring his daughter's marriage prospects for life.

Kulsum, Hamid's wife, was a beautiful, moody woman fifteen years his junior from his hometown of Chapai Nawabganj in northwestern Bangladesh. She had joined the Qureshi household staff after marrying Hamid, and had borne three children. Their sons were married with children of their own, grandkids that Hamid and Kulsum were grandparents to largely in name only. Through Qureshi's connections, the sons lived and worked in Dubai. Hamid had named their daughter Shiuli, after the flowers he'd been staring at while Kulsum was in labor.

Kulsum too had become a bag of nerves of late, made all the worse by Hamid's deepening angst. Dragging around during the day, worry-freighted and sapped of energy, her anxiety was starting to affect her work around the house and her behavior toward their daughter. She picked at everything Shiuli did, finding one fault after another, until one afternoon the girl broke down. Kulsum told her to go hide her face for shame, because if such little criticism undid her, she was in for a lifetime of misery as a daughter-in-law and wife.

"She's done nothing wrong," said Hamid.

Kulsum said, "Nothing will be right with her either, if she remains unmarried much longer, and is treated like she's a little girl."

"And when were you so miserable as my wife? My parents never looked at you but with blessings," said Hamid.

Shiuli would overhear her parents from the adjoining room in the servants' quarters as if it were someone else's life being planned and discussed, and she were merely an eavesdropper.

A few days later, Hamid brought the matter to his employer. He served Harun Qureshi's dinner himself, instead of letting the cook do it, and spoke at length while Qureshi ate. Qureshi listened to Hamid without interruption, inquiry or surprise. He wondered why it had taken this long for Hamid to bring the matter up. He finished eating and moved to the living room. Smoking and going through the day's newspapers, he continued listening.

"I have my savings for her dowry," Hamid went on. "It should be enough, I think."

"Dowry?" Harun Qureshi spoke for the first time in nearly an hour. Hamid had thinly recounted his life and times since his beginnings in Qureshi's service, his marriage, the birth of his children, the good fortune bestowed by Qureshi on his two sons, and the final act that would see to his daughter's future. "You've found a boy already? When did all this happen?"

"He's the son of a childhood friend from home. Made quite a good life for himself and his family from what his father left him."

"He's your friend and he expects a dowry?"

Hamid shook his head irritably. "In these matters, no one is a friend. You have friends in business. Are they friendly in matters of money?"

Harun Qureshi folded the paper he was skimming and set it on the coffee table.

"No, they're not," he said. "Not even family is family in matters of money." The reference, Hamid knew, was to his third cousin, Waseem Qureshi, the industrialist tycoon. The cousins had spent most of their acquaintance with each other as foes in business since a joint venture early in their careers went asunder. Each believed the other one owed him capital from the lost investment. As older men they'd become two feuding lifelong bachelors with nothing else to keep them occupied.

"Whatever I have I will give," Hamid said.

"If you need help, just tell me." But Harun Qureshi knew his old housekeeper well. Hamid would rather spend all night trying to navigate his pride than be forthright at the cost of compromising it. Qureshi snuffed out his cigarette in the ashtray and pushed himself to his feet. "Come inside."

Hamid waited by the bedroom door while Harun Qureshi went to the steel almirah that stood in a corner. Qureshi extracted a small box draped with a purple silk handkerchief. He set it on the bed, removed the handkerchief, and opened the box like it was a treasure chest he'd discovered after a lifetime's search. He gave the contents a once-over and motioned for Hamid to come take a look.

"This is my mother's wedding jewelry," Harun Qureshi said. "The last of it. She left most of it to my three sisters. This was for when I got married. Unless it's buried with me, I'm not taking it anywhere." He closed the box and placed the handkerchief over it. "It will be in here whenever you're ready. As far as money is concerned, whatever your friend asks you for, don't say no."

"I've eaten your salt. So have my wife and children. What you did for my sons to enjoy good lives, I will never be able to repay."

"Okay, okay, now go. Give yourself some peace of mind."

Kulsum expected her husband to run to her with a round-up of his discussion with the master, but as soon as she asked Hamid about it he shunned her. For the rest of the day, she in turn was short with him. The few times he asked her something she told him he could figure it out himself as he was so smart and full of secrets. Hamid finally gave in when Kulsum took it out on their daughter, scolding the girl to take her dinner to her bedroom and not eat it shamelessly in front of the cook, the driver, and the night guard, as Shiuli had been doing since she was a child.

"She's not a child anymore," Kulsum said sternly, as though her decision needed a final seal.

After dinner Hamid entered their room, and found Kulsum cleaning the floor with a broom, every swipe a big, forceful strike aimed at an unseen qualm.

"Okay, my God, okay. Put away that broom and sit down before you choke me to death with that dust." He coughed.

"I clean that big house all day and my own sleeping space gets neglected," Kulsum complained.

"This room is also part of his house."

Kulsum glared at her husband and threw the broom into a corner. "What do you want? Why are you bothering me?"

They could hear the loud splashing of water from the latrine where Shiuli was taking a bath as Hamid told Kulsum of his conversation with the master.

"It must be pure gold, no?" asked Kulsum, bug-eyed with interest, her daylong veneer of anger gone.

"Heaven help this woman. Of all things, that's where your mind goes," Hamid said. "What do you think? A man like him will have a cabinet full of fake jewelry?"

"Cabinet-full!"

"Listen to me. Helal Sobhan has been writing to me for some time now. He's become a very powerful man, and he has a son, his youngest."

"She could be happy there, under the right circumstances," Kulsum said without enthusiasm.

"She will go where her husband wants. I'm going to write to Helal and tell him I'm ready to finalize things."

The sound of water had stopped in the latrine. Hamid called for Shiuli, whom they could hear humming next door, and she came to their door.

"Come here," said Hamid. "Your marriage has been fixed. You're no longer a child, and life won't treat you like one forever."

Shiuli fell at her mother's feet, pushing her face in to her lap, crying, her wet hair in ropy tangles.

"Stop it, you stupid girl," said Kulsum. "I got married. My mother before me got married, and so will your own daughter someday. Get up."

Hamid took her chin in his hand, and he told her, "I will bring you a prince."

"Don't tell her nonsense like that." Kulsum pushed his hand away. "Now listen," she said to Shiuli, "from now on until your wedding day you will stay in here, and when you're out make sure I can still see you. I don't want to see you skipping around the house like you're five years old. Apart from your father, men are men, and that goes for the master too. Do you hear me? Don't make me make it harder for you. I will, you know. Now go. Dry your hair before you catch a deathly cold."

Hamid lit a beedi and stretched out in bed. "No need to be so harsh with her."

"There is every need," Kulsum answered back. "Now you tell me, what kind of jewelry is it?"

"The kind," Hamid said, letting smoke waft from his nose and mouth, "that you and I couldn't buy or own over ten generations."

Kulsum snorted haughtily, lay down, and turned on her side, facing away from him. "I want my sons here," her voice was low and shaky. "It's been so long. You had to force them to go away. Those witches they married are seeing to it that we never see them again. My grandchildren are probably being told that their grandmother is dead."

Hamid inhaled the beedi into his lungs. "Yes, yes, I've drowned my family in nothing but despair. How will I ever show my sinful face to God?"

Kulsum ignored the sarcasm, mumbling curses at her daughters-in-law and their low birth. Her one-time excitement over them had given way to hate after a quarrel before they left for Dubai; they had overheard Kulsum telling her sons that they must always obey her first. The wives, Kulsum held, had united against her. Now they would forever be monsters out for her blood, and the blood of her poor, simple sons.

After the initial exchange of letters in which Hamid confirmed his wish for their children to be married, Helal Sobhan, as Hamid had expected, mentioned that they should meet in person. He was, in fact, happy at the prospect of the wedding taking place in Chapai Nawabganj, the place of his birth, the place he envisioned when he thought of home, no matter how much of his life he had lived in Dhaka. At least one contingent of his grandchildren would someday be born in the home of their ancestors.

Three days later Hamid left by bus for Chapai Nawabganj. The journey was murderous on his bones; by the time he got off the bus, he felt as though he had just escaped torture. A loud, raspy voice growled his name, laughing. Hamid saw a fat, squat man with graying oily hair and a huge belly standing in front of a dust-covered red Toyota Corolla. His bushy groomed beard had been hennaed red since his pilgrimage to Mecca. But for his face Helal Sobhan looked nothing like the bandy-legged boy that Hamid remembered from their childhood, the boy who looked malnourished all the time, no matter how much of a glutton he was.

"Old friend, this is a great occasion," Sobhan clasped his arms around Hamid's thin frame and gave his ribs a crushing embrace. A driver took Hamid's bag and put it in the trunk. Sobhan ushered him into the car, and then they were weaving through traffic that looked to Hamid no different from the crush of bodies and dust and wheels of Dhaka.

Helal Sobhan's house, a two-story building, was a thirty-minute drive from the bus stop. The second floor was dark, unlike the first, which was lit up like a hotel. Hamid wondered if that was where his Shiuli would live with her new husband. He was also struck with the realization for the first time that his little girl would be so far away. He controlled his face so that it did not betray his fears, even as he felt the downward pull at the corners of his mouth and the heat behind his eyes.

Hamid hadn't said a word during the drive while Helal Sobhan regaled him with updates about himself, the town, life as it had changed, the good and the despicable, with no in-between state of affairs, and how the time had long ago arrived for the system to be shaken up. It all came to Hamid as though he were underwater, the garbled, muffled sound of his old friend's voice reaching him as he sank unstoppably toward the bottomless depth.

"So? Back home again," Sobhan's voice ruptured Hamid's reveries. They were in a living room brightly lit and cramped with furniture, most of which was covered with oilcloth and large sheets of multicolored and flower-patterned plastic. Sobhan was next to him on a three-seater sofa, and across from them was a middle-aged woman, wiry thin, with bad teeth, pale skin, and stringy hair pulled tautly back under the head-covering made of the remainder of her sari. Beside her sat a frail young man with a round face and oily skin, and hands that were like a child's. He was a miniature Helal Sobhan.

"My wife and my youngest, my boy Shahjahan. Boy, stand up, touch Uncle's feet and get his blessings."

Mrs. Sobhan salaamed shyly. Shahjahan did as he was told, catching Hamid off-guard. Hamid reacted with the customary gesture to show Shahjahan that there was no need to touch his feet, and offered his blessings with a palm held over the boy's head.

"Okay, now you two get out of here," Helal Sobhan dismissed his family. "We old friends have a lot to talk about and catching up to do." His laughter rattled in his chest like marbles in a tin can, followed by a phlegm-filled fit of coughing. Mrs. Sobhan and Shahjahan obeyed and left. "Come, my friend. We'll walk on my lawn out back and talk. Stale air bothers my lungs, even in my own house."

The night was clear, the full moon close to the horizon low and plump. Sobhan led them to the edge of the property under a large tamarind tree outlined by the dim light of the moon like a hovering ghoul. Hamid had not seen so much uninterrupted land and sky since he had been a child around here, and now his heart grew heavy again, his eyes stung. He muted a sniffle under a loud coughing and clearing of his throat.

"I can't tell you how fortuitous this is," said Sobhan. "I wish you had more daughters so I could have married them to my two other sons. I couldn't tell you many things in my letters, you know, not easy, not safe either. Things of a sensitive nature."

"I was surprised to hear from you at first, after all these years, but then I took it as a good sign," said Hamid. "I guess I didn't think much about what else you were saying. It was confusing."

"Good, good, good. I will make everything clear. Shahjahan is a good, obedient boy. He's a little slow at times, but that's his mother's fault. She treats him like a baby still, but all that is going to stop. As soon as he's a husband and father. You like him?"

"He is—a fine looking boy—" Hamid's chest burned, words clogged up and dissipated before reaching his mouth.

"That's good, that's very good," Sobhan clapped Hamid's back. "Look, we're old friends, like brothers, and we're about to become family for real, so I'll be frank. There are opportunities, for both of us that I can see to. All this," he waved an arm behind him indicating his home and everyone and everything in it, "pales in comparison."

"You've done well, by the grace of God. Your father was a smart man."

"What he left was a drop in the bucket to what I've built, and still have to achieve. If my father had done what yours did, and bundled us off to Dhaka back then, I would have made something of things there. But it was meant to happen here, where I belong. Look here, I have the respect and the ear of the people here. District elections are three months away. I'm going to run, and I'm going to win." He grinned wide and proud. Hamid caught a whiff of alcohol on him he hadn't noticed before. "Think of the life and respect your daughter will have."

"When do you see the wedding happening?" Hamid asked.

"Yes, yes, that's why it's imperative that I win this election, so we can move things along."

"I see."

"Listen here. Things have a way of happening. I don't need to tell you, you've lived all your life in Dhaka. You know. I can have this election in the palm of my hands, no contest. But it will not come cheap."

"I don't understand politics. Whatever you say, I'm sure you know best. And the people too who will vote for you."

Helal Sobhan shook his head, frustrated. "To hell with the people and their votes. Let them vote till their fingers fall off. It won't do me any damn good. I'm sure you have a dowry set aside for your only daughter, no?"

"Can I have a glass of water?"

"Of course. This is your house. You can have anything you like. You and me, my friend, we will own whatever we want, whoever we want. Now. About the dowry. What have you set aside?"

"I've had a long journey," Hamid said.

"You worry me, not giving a straight answer. Just tell me that you've planned adequately. Because I have. And everything depends on this."

Hamid could say no more. His chest and throat and mouth felt coated with cotton. Lightheaded, unsure of who he was talking to anymore, or about what, Hamid asked to be shown where he could sleep for the night. Sobhan huffed back into the house, Hamid following, and shouted for a servant to show the guest to his room. Hamid went to bed without being offered dinner.

In the morning Sobhan was different, warmer, briefly apologetic. A lavish breakfast was waiting at the table when Hamid, worn with worry and the sleepless night, came out, prepared for the worst news. Mrs. Sobhan and Shahjahan sat on one side of the table. Helal Sobhan occupied the head chair. He greeted Hamid with all the enthusiasm he had brought to the bus station the day before, stood up, and pulled out a chair for him. He poured him tea, spoke jovially about the years that had passed while Hamid lived in Dhaka, the changes, good and bad, their childhood spent carefree in a way that children today would never know.

Hamid could barely keep down a few sips of tea. Sobhan shoveled down three fried eggs, half a dozen pieces of buttered toast, a glass of milk, belched, and told his family to leave them alone.

"So. Everything is final then," he said when they were gone. "Last night you were tired from your journey. You've had time to sleep and think about things. I'm sure you want the best for your daughter."

"I have to catch the afternoon bus back," said Hamid. "Just tell me what's on your mind. Let's not prolong things if they're going nowhere."

"Oh, my old friend," Sobhan chortled, "sounding like a citified man, all bustle and rush in your blood. Did I say anything about things going nowhere? Have some sense. I only said that big plans need appropriate investment in them."

"I wasn't aware of your political career in the making as part of the wedding of our children."

"Everything is connected, Abdul Hamid. Life is a series of connections. Listen here, if I don't win this election, there will be no wedding, and you will never find a boy for your daughter from here to the farthest tip of North Bengal. Imagine the shame, Abdul Hamid. Think about the poor girl instead of your big head and ego."

Hamid reached home, and refused to speak with Kulsum or look Shiuli in the face. In the morning, while Harun Qureshi drank tea, Hamid told him about his trip and the pertinent parts of the conversation that passed between him and Helal Sobhan.

"And you still want your daughter to be married to this man's son?"

"It's a matter of my name."

"Very well. I said I would help in any way. What do you need? How much?"

"My year's salary. That should be enough. You can make it an advance."

"That's a senseless idea. Take the gold, take the money."

"It will be an advance," Hamid insisted. Qureshi knew arguing would be futile.

Later that night, Kulsum finally cornered him. Hamid was selective about how much he told her but whatever she heard she liked. She called Shiuli into their room, who promptly broke into tears.

"You were such a happy little girl. What is it with all this crying now in the face of this good news?" Kulsum said. "First thing in the morning we will go and seek blessings from sahib."

Harun Qureshi was not good with formalities that were not connected to business. He offered his congratulations to Hamid and Kulsum, and gave a five-hundred taka note to Shiuli. which Kulsum's hand intercepted like a flitting sparrow, plucking the note before their daughter could take it.

"No, no, too much, this is too much," Hamid protested. Qureshi stood his ground and waved him off. Kulsum had already stowed the note somewhere about herself. Hamid's desire was to have Harun Qureshi as an honored guest at the wedding. He almost mentioned it, with the request teetering on the tip of his tongue, but held back, panicking at the thought of Helal Sobhan causing a disaster by his behavior. He told his wife and daughter to go back to the servants' quarters.

"My mind is made up," he told Harun Qureshi. "If I'm going to see her married before I die, it has to happen now. Whether the money is enough or not, I will deal with it."

"I told you already, the amount is not a problem."

"It is to me."

"Okay. Rahman will be coming to the house tomorrow evening. I'll have him get the check ready and bring it with him. It's not my business, but I've added a little extra. This nonsense dowry business should be outlawed. It's criminal."

"What to do?" Hamid said.

Next evening when the accountant arrived, Harun Qureshi called for Hamid. Rahman was a belligerent man in his mid-fifties, a heavy drinker of cheap local liquor, brusque to the point of being at times unbearable to the other employees in Harun Qureshi's staff, but devoted to his work. In fifteen years he had never called in sick and Qureshi had never had occasion to question his work. There was talk among the business elite of Dhaka that Waseem Qureshi was facing a possible audit by the Anti-Corruption Commission. All Harun Qureshi could think of was Rahman in a room with ACC men, blasting them with impunity when they questioned the veracity of his work.

Rahman brought out the check from his briefcase and set it on the coffee table, deliberately leaving the handing over of it to Hamid for his boss. Qureshi picked it up, and, holding it, said, "If this is not enough—"

"It will have to be," Hamid said. "The formalities have to be done still. I have to take them with me to Chapai Nawabganj."

"There are others in this house that can do extra work for a few days," said Qureshi. "Come and go as you need. Just keep me informed."

Hamid bowed his head. He caught Rahman out of the corner of his eye, scowling purse-lipped.

"When are you leaving?" Qureshi asked.

"As soon as I hear back from the boy's father," Hamid replied.

"Good."

"This will be taken out of my salary," said Hamid. "All of it."

"We'll worry about that later when the time comes."

Walking away toward the kitchen, Hamid was still within earshot to hear Rahman grumble to Harun Qureshi, "You're too liberal, sir. These days even generosity has a big price."

Hamid did not stay around to hear Harun Qureshi's response.

Time moved faster than arrangements could be made, and within the month the wedding was confirmed. Helal Sobhan pressed Hamid for the exact amount of the dowry until the last moment, and stepped back appeased when Hamid mentioned the gold jewelry that was part of the package. To him too, as he had done with Kulsum, Hamid imparted as much information as was necessary, leaving out the possibility that, even though Harun Qureshi had not asked for the jewelry back, Hamid's intention was to return it. In that regard things felt tentative, which was troubling, but at least they were moving forward.

On a dazzling, hot morning, Hamid boarded a bus with his wife and daughter, the box of jewelry from Harun Qureshi wrapped inside a prayer mat and pressed to his body. The other luggage they had was a small metal trunk that Kulsum had stuffed with nearly every article of clothing the three of them owned. Harun Qureshi's driver dropped them off at the bus stop.

On the journey, during a lull when most of the passengers were asleep, Hamid woke from troubled slumber to find

Shiuli caressing the covered box wedged between them. On Shiuli's other side Kulsum was snoring with her head against the window. Hamid touched Shiuli's hand and tried to smile.

"Is he really a prince?" Shiuli asked. Hamid patted her head, closed his eyes and tilted his face to motion for her to sleep.

The same red Toyota Corolla was waiting at the bus stop, without Helal Sobhan to welcome them. This time the driver made no effort to help with the luggage, but popped open the trunk from inside and waited impatiently behind the wheel.

Helal Sobhan's house was chaotic with workmen shouting, hammers banging, lights being strung up and down and across every inch of it, food smells wafting out of the kitchen, and, it seemed to Hamid and his family, the entire neighborhood. Children ran around shrieking. Mostly men and a few women alongside their husbands went in and out of the house, and inside, there were people crammed to capacity in every room, doing exactly what was presently beyond speculation. Mostly they were eating, chatting with each other, and eating some more. At times the house sounded like a crowded mosque after Eid prayers, the hum of men's voices buzzing around like electric current. Kulsum's face was fixed in a smile, Shiuli's in indifference. Inside Hamid pumped a heavy heart.

The festivities confused Hamid, until they were inside and learned the reason. A servant showed them to an office past the living room, and there Helal Sobhan sat at a desk in the center of a circle of men. The conversation stopped when Hamid and his family entered. The men looked up, plain-faced and dour. Sobhan greeted Hamid with the volume and flair of a king, happy and seemingly unaware of what was happening in his kingdom outside his castle.

"Come in, come in, no time for formalities!" Sobhan took Hamid by the shoulders and pulled him into an embrace, once more testing the strength of Hamid's ribcage. He salamed Kulsum, and gave Shiuli a look of sudden disgust. "Everyone, go from here, go, go get more food. I'll be out in a while."

The men filed out of the room bowing, smiling, leaving behind words of encouragement and cheer. "Sit down, sit down," Sobhan pointed to chairs strewn around the room. He called for his wife, and within seconds Mrs. Sobhan had slipped quietly into the room. "Take them away," Sobhan indicated Kulsum and Shiuli. Hamid watched as his wife and daughter were led away, fearful, despite knowing better, that that was the last time he would see them.

"All these people, they're not here already for the wedding, are they?" Hamid asked.

Helal Sobhan laughed, phlegm squelching in this chest. "My constituents. Not only constituents, but the men that will enable my victory. The mullahs you saw are connected to Jamaat, and the student Shibir support comes with that, which is big, they're both major sources of support. I know you know this living in Dhaka. The influence that carries with those people. Three of them in that group you just saw are related to the police superintendent. You see the kind of respect and adoration that awaits? This is only the beginning. And these preparations serve a dual purpose. The election and the wedding."

Only the last part registered with Hamid. The rest were dull blows.

"So, all this is for the wedding, too—" said Hamid.

Sobhan settled into his chair, stroked his double chin, and said, "Your girl, she's rather plain, isn't she? Not the prettiest thing. Unlike your wife. Too tall I think for a girl, and too thin."

"She's a very good girl," Hamid said, resentfully.

"Of course. I'm sure she is. Is that what you were talking about?"

Hamid followed Sobhan's glinting eyes to the jewelry box under his arm.

"Of course," Sobhan grinned, "along with the money."

"There's more to this than just jewelry for my daughter's wedding," said Hamid. "This jewelry comes from a very special person."

"You're such a sentimental old fellow. Let's see it."

After ogling the contents of the box, Sobhan wanted to see proof of the money. Hamid handed him the folded check, which Sobhan read with disappointment.

"Is this all?" said Sobhan.

"It's more than a year's salary. I cannot do any more."

"Keep your voice down."

"How much more do you need? Is any of it going to go to the children at all? Or is it all for your—politics?"

"Don't be so judgmental," Sobhan huffed petulantly. "Life costs money. And this is only a check."

"Cash it. The money is there."

"I will. Tomorrow we will go to the bank." The two men stared at each other, and then, as if somehow capable of reading Hamid's thoughts, Sobhan smiled: "In money matters even family comes second."

For the rest of the evening Kulsum remained slack-jawed and wide-eyed. Shiuli quietly lay in the large bed she occupied with her mother, turned away, intermittently crying, and, finally, late at night, after the festivities outside subsided to the chirp of crickets, frog croaks thumping the warm night air, and dogs baying in the distance, drifted into sleep. Hamid took the second, smaller bed on the other side of the room. Such a large house, so much at his feet, and still Sobhan had to have more. More money, with which he would do god-knows-what; grease more palms, buy more people, get fatter.

The voice of his wife cut through Hamid's worries for more than an hour, until he told her to shut up. She whined that he was a sour, bad luck charm and nudged Shiuli, criticizing her for being ungrateful in the face of such luxury and comfort awaiting her, who shunned her even from the depths of sleep. Kulsum continued grumbling until her words dwindled into snoring.

Hamid dozed on and off for a while, his worries shocking him awake like a vindictive warden each time rest descended. He could hear faint chatter from just outside their room, which was at the back of the house, on the rear lawn. The rest of the house was quiet. Hamid removed the covers and swung his legs over the edge of the bed.

"Baba?" Shiuli mumbled. Hamid went to her. Her sleep was deep, exhausted, as if it were the first time she was resting after years of grinding toil. Hamid drew the covers over her.

"Where are you going?" Kulsum asked, as Hamid made his way to the door.

"Woman, I have to go the bathroom, for god's sake. Go back to sleep."

Silence lay over the house like it had been abandoned, the ruckus of a few hours ago a distant, unremarkable memory. The chatter on the rear lawn had also ceased. Hamid made his way in the dark toward the bathroom, which was down the hallway near the kitchen. The cool

floor sent chills through his feet and up his back. The smell
of food hung stale in the air and he realized he wanted a
glass of water more than he needed to use the bathroom,
so he rounded the corner and went into the kitchen. For a
moment, he imagined he heard voices. All the activity, the
sounds and the multitude of conversations from earlier in
the day, echoed in his head. He found a glass and drank in
the darkness, grateful for the privacy, the silence. He was
at the door when a gasp, and stifled laughter, stopped him
short. Instinctively, he reached for the wall and flipped on
a switch.

Smarting from the shock of sudden light his vision
focused like a camera lens, wavered, blurred, searched
for clarity, found it, and the hazy edges around the world
sharpened. The tube lights on the ceiling flickered and
clicked and stabilized, raining their cold, blue phospho-
rescence on Shahjahan, naked, except for a pair of white
underpants, on all fours with his mouth open and hanging
over the groin of another young man in a tank top, who
was a few years older than him and stripped bare from the
waist down. Hamid's entrance did nothing to stir them, as
if a bee had droned in and caused a moment's undesired but
bearable pause. Shahjahan's quiet, dreamy, opinion-less
eyes looked at Hamid, moved to his companion's, and he
continued.

"Now we can proceed," Helal Sobhan's mouth spread
in the widest smile Hamid had yet seen him don. His
cheeks puffed and the corners of his eyes crinkled. He
clutched the briefcase he'd brought along for the cash,
patted it, and shook the bank manager's hand.

"Old friend," Sobhan said to Hamid when they were in
the car driving back to the house, "you gave me a scare, but

I knew you were too good not to stand by your word. It's the kind of people we are from around here. Honest, salt of the earth, men of our word. And that is exactly the philosophy with which I will clean up this place. Cheer up, old man. You see that this is not one but two great occasions we're celebrating."

People and workers had begun crawling all over and around the house since dawn. The banging and the shouting had resumed. As soon as the car entered the driveway, the group of men from yesterday converged on Helal Sobhan, greeting him like a deity. Hamid slipped out and made a quick escape inside.

Kulsum had woken refreshed and chatty, and pestered Shiuli out of sleep to get her ready. Hamid came in and sat on the edge of his bed.

"Well?" Kulsum said.

"What's the matter, Baba?" asked Shiuli.

"Quiet," Kulsum told her.

"He has what he wants," said Hamid.

"Allah's mercy!" Kulsum sighed, and continued putting the final touches to Shiuli.

Through the closed window Hamid heard the workers talking. He opened a shutter. They were about twenty feet away. With them was the man Hamid had seen with Shahjahan. He had on the same tank top and lungi. By daylight he looked younger, glowing like polished teak. Sweat glistened on his arms and shoulders, the muscles pulsing under his sun-seared skin with every movement. Their eyes passed over each other. Hamid shut the window.

By lunchtime the house was in the same frenzy of building and work as the day before. Men streamed in and out like devotees to and from a house of worship. Helal Sobhan held court in his office, loud and laughing, fed by the encouragement and support being lavished on him, until his two older sons arrived, and he postponed the business of politics for lunch.

He talked throughout the meal. His other sons had come without their families, for which Mrs. Sobhan briefly and meekly admonished them. Sobhan scolded her into silence.

"They're here for more important business than lugging around a wife and kids where there's no need for them."

"They would have liked to have come," the eldest, Shahriar, said.

"Nonsense," Sobhan interrupted. "They'll be here for the wedding. Otherwise all they'll do is take up space."

Suleiman, the second son, said, "How can there be space for your family with all these strangers in here? Who are these people?"

"Boy, don't tell me who I can have in my house," Sobhan warned. "Keep your mouth shut until you're told to speak. You see this?" he addressed Hamid. "Everything they have is because of their father, and now they sit at my table and challenge me."

"Keep your mouth shut," Shahriar told Suleiman.

"I said nothing wrong," Suleiman protested.

"Talk sense into your stupid brother," Sobhan told Shahriar. "Don't make me do it."

Shahjahan sat at the far end of the table, next to his mother, and during the meal never raised his eyes. He was so unlike his brothers it would not be a stretch to presume he was adopted. Kulsum had placed Shiuli strategically across from him. Shiuli stole a few glances at him, which went unreturned.

After lunch Shahriar and Suleiman went upstairs. Hamid heard the older sons grumbling to each other. Helal Sobhan thumped back to his office having announced that the wedding should be gotten over with within a fortnight at the latest; he had more pressing business that needed his time. Mrs. Sobhan approached Kulsum fearfully and asked quietly to speak with her in private. Kulsum ordered Shiuli to go to their room and stay there. Shahjahan, already fidgety during the meal, made his getaway as soon as his father was out of sight. The dining room emptied out with the urgency of a forced evacuation. Hamid, concerned about Shiuli, wishing to know her mind for once in the absence of her mother, went to their room and found her sitting on the bed, her head leaning back, staring at the ceiling.

"How are you?" he asked from the doorway. "You didn't eat much."

"Baba," she said, without turning to him, "he's not a prince."

From the front of the house came the thuds of a lone hammer on wood. Most of the loud, busy work had been paused for the afternoon. Hamid listened for the workers on the back lawn. He went to the end of the hallway to the door leading out to the lawn. When he tried it, it opened.

The sun was fierce, the afternoon burning in its unforgiving fire. The shadiest section was under the tamarind tree, and there the men rested, cooling their heads and heated bodies, smoking in the silence of their post-meal lethargy.

Off to one side, separated from them, were Shahjahan and his companion. The others were paying them no mind. Shahjahan's head was down, his knees drawn up with his arms hugged around them. They were talking to each other inconspicuously. His companion was doing most of the talking. Shahjahan mostly shook his head as though in defiance of everything he heard. And then he started laughing. He threw his head back. His arms unlocked and fell behind him supporting his weight. His legs straightened out. The laughter floated to Hamid's ear and for a moment he had the mad impulse to laugh along with Shahjahan, to laugh until the entire house heard him. Then Hamid closed the door and, accepting what was to come, turned toward Helal Sobhan's office.

The Happy Widow

Rosie Moyeen's neighbor across the hallway, Mrs. Zaheer, turned off the stove and poured freshly brewed ginger tea into two cups. She repeated her favorite stories to Rosie—about her first husband, a bastard of the highest order, and the second, a gambling, philandering louse. Laughing would have been a perfectly appropriate response, but Rosie still felt it wrong, no matter how many times she heard these stories. She pressed her lips and accepted the tea. Mrs. Zaheer pulled back the chair adjacent to Rosie at the small kitchen table and encouraged her to laugh. The reason Rosie thought laughter inappropriate was because, like Mr. Moyeen, both Mrs. Zaheer's ex- husbands were dead.

The philanderer had left Mrs. Zaheer with gambling debts, and the bastard with a son she adored. He was around the same age as Rosie. Each time Mrs. Zaheer mentioned him, a glint flashed through her eyes, but just as suddenly dimmed.

Mrs. Zaheer was a large, big-breasted, full-boned seventy-year-old with a deep voice like a man's, thick, strong hands, unlined facial skin, and white hair perfectly drawn back into a bun. Around her Rosie felt like a little girl; she became tentative in speech and movement, and was preternaturally awestruck.

"But that wife of his," said Mrs. Zaheer, "I don't know. What more can I tell you?"

That wife of her son's was never called by a name, and Mrs. Zaheer always stopped at the same point.

"When did you see them—him last?"

"Too long ago," Mrs. Zaheer sighed, which Rosie found not entirely genuine. "It's not up to him." Mrs. Zaheer circled the rim of her mug with a finger. "He's my boy, though. No matter what or who there is between us. He proved it, long before he was a grown man. He saved my life."

Mr. Moyeen had been an exemplary husband. He had never raised his voice at Rosie, let alone his hand. When Rosie first heard the stories of Mrs. Zaheer's first husband chasing her around the house with a butcher's knife she tried to imagine Mr. Moyeen doing the same, but the idea of it was too absurd to even conjure an image. The scar running down the back of Mrs. Zaheer's right arm, however—straight and vicious-looking even to this day, thirty years later—was no laughing matter. "If my Kamran hadn't been there that night—" Mrs. Zaheer would trail off, then shake her head, chuckle, and repeat her favorite phrase to Rosie. "There are great advantages to being a widow."

She never elaborated exactly what those advantages were, or what they could mean for someone other than her. Rosie accepted that at the point Mrs. Zaheer had reached in life, she expected others to just get it, to understand her celebration of the deaths of not one but two insufferable husbands. In Dhaka, no matter how bad the husbands were, it was the women who were gossiped about, maligned, condemned as shrews who had driven their men to untimely deaths.

Each time Rosie left Mrs. Zaheer's flat, she felt she should be wiser, but was not. Mrs. Zaheer was masterful with phrases, her most recent coinage being "There are great advantages to being a widow." Rosie thought she should make a poster with it, start a club for likeminded widows and make it their official motto. When her mind, coaxed by Mrs. Zaheer's widowed triumphalism, got swept too far in mistaken camaraderie, Rosie felt disloyal. Her husband had been a gentle, soft-spoken, soft hearted soul. He deserved better than pithy phrases. Certainly better than being made the butt of flippant jokes and recriminations. Rosie's memories of him held nothing but times that any woman would envy. If Mrs. Zaheer had seen them together when he was alive, she would have reconsidered her general bitterness towards men.

Rosie accepted that Mrs. Zaheer had every reason to be celebratory about her husbands' deaths, for reveling in the advantages of widowhood. But she also wished that her anger weren't so all-consuming. Ultimately, it shouldn't matter to Rosie what Mrs. Zaheer thought and felt, any more than it should matter that Dhaka gossip had painted Rosie as the devil who had ended the life of her accomplished husband, who had been in the army and then the civil service, and was once the most sought-after bachelor in the city. Rosie's parents received notes of congratulation for a whole year after the wedding, each with an undercurrent of resentment slightly stronger than the one before. Rosie's father loved reading them out loud and then tearing them up.

Their wedding festivities had lasted a week. They had taken place at Rosie's parents' home before they had had to sell it to developers fifteen years later, for it to be demolished and built into a high rise building. During that week Rosie felt she had been transported to another land. Amidst the lights and the music that were always turned on and that played round-the-clock, Rosie forgot she was in the same house in which she was born. Captain Akbar Moyeen, in uniform, glittering and blinking with medals, finally sat next to his new wife in the back of the Toyota that was decked with strings of marigolds and white roses, and the couple was driven the fifteen minutes to the flat where, two decades later, Mr. Moyeen would leave the new Mrs. Rosie Moyeen widowed.

Kind Mr. Moyeen, likable Mr. Moyeen, respectful and gracious Mr. Moyeen, charitable, honest, and good. Good, yes, good; so good that, a year into her marriage to him, Rosie went through a period of waking in the night weeping. She would clench her teeth and lock herself in the bathroom so she could sob her heart out. The way he loved her scared her, the way a woman beaten nightly by her husband is terrified of his footsteps coming up the stairs. Mr. Moyeen's goodness nauseated Rosie with dread. Even when they learned that she could never bear children, Mr. Moyeen draped his long, muscle-knotted arm around her and held her all the way home from the doctor's office. Then he took her on holiday to Nepal.

His illness had been sudden. One day he was robust, doing his morning pushups and jogging three times a week, and the next he couldn't keep down his food or walk without breaking down in tears from the pain. Going against everything he was, had spent his life being, Akbar Moyeen had to take to his bed for his last two years on earth, except for a dozen or so steps every day to keep blood clots and bedsores at bay. Rosie had the opportunity to devote her time and existence to him. There it was. The way out. To be as good, or at least try to be, as he had been to her. It was a chance to show, if not her love then a form of love, but the army doctor assigned a personal caregiver, saying that it would be the best option since Mr. Moyeen refused to spend his remaining days in a hospital bed. That took away the last channel through which Rosie could return his devotion, leaving her only the privacy of their nights to hold his hand and talk to him. But by then the day had taken its toll, and Akbar Moyeen would drift into sleep, or as Rosie feared every night, into death.

During the day Rosie would stand by like a novice, watching the young caregiver, an army medic, who told her that he had wanted to be a singer but his father had beaten him and dragged him to the enlistment center, tend to her husband's every need. She watched him hold her husband around the waist and help him walk. They went up and down the rear veranda twice, which left Mr. Moyeen trembling and wincing from the effort. The medic would then massage his feet and give him orange juice. For two years the young medic was there from six in the morning until after dinner, never sitting for a meal, and waiting by his charge's bed until he was satisfactorily certain his work was done. The morning Mr. Moyeen didn't wake up, Rosie waited for the medic, and when she told him, she felt like the outsider giving the news to a family member. And yet, Rosie envied his detachment.

She asked him, as the truck carrying her husband's body growled and lumbered precariously out of the driveway on its way to the Banani graveyard, how he managed it, the detachment, and did it ever stay with him afterward, the sickness and the death, the time lost? Did it affect his ability even for a short time to function properly? His answer stuck with Rosie. His father, the medic told her, had died coughing blood and cursing his mother, his brother, his sister, and him, and they had all cared for him till the end, accepting his abuse, which—when he could no longer spew in words—leaked out of him in blood. At that point his father had enough hate in him for them all, and they were too numbed by it to be able to feel more than a sense of obligation toward caring for him. It came from a place not of love but of being deprived of any choice. At that point he was within a few months of his service coming to an end, and Rosie asked if he would go back to his dream of being a singer. She remembered the military nurse's quiet laugh, the shy look at the ground before he told her that he was thinking of re-enlisting. Rosie had the impulse to talk him out of it. The medic wished her well, and left.

Mr. Moyeen's illness—which exhausted and defied the prognoses of three army doctors, including Dr Menon's, Mr. Moyeen's primary physician and friend since they were six years old—stalked Rosie like a crazed ex-husband or lover. It was sudden, true, there was no doubt. Dr Menon had devoted all his time to Akbar Moyeen. He kept himself on call for Rosie round the clock. He arranged for the medic, and advised Rosie not to forget her own health. He even wept one night. Akbar was the better soldier, the stronger athlete, the more brilliant student, and the greater human being. What did life have against such a man that it had plunged into his system its mysterious message of destruction? From where? Out of what? Rosie mentioned the doctor's anguish to her husband, and the next time he was there, Mr. Moyeen made Dr Menon do twenty-five pushups, and the two of them laughed, and called for Rosie to join them. It was the only time Rosie saw Mr. Moyeen reprimand anyone. Sudden. Rosie saw the crazed ex-lover wielding the word like a sword above its head, crashing around the flat in pursuit of her.

Mrs. Zaheer moved into her flat the year after Mr. Moyeen died, and so never saw Rosie and him together to give their marriage its space in her judgment. All marriages were false pretenses for terror and unhappiness. If Mrs. Zaheer would accept a phrase from Rosie, that would be Rosie's contribution. Betrayal, too, Rosie could add to it. Mrs. Zaheer, without asking or confirming, would assume the betrayal to be the doing of Mr. Moyeen.

Rosie was happy, and relieved, that instead of a couple or a family, another widow had moved in across the hall. The flat below her had been newly filled by a couple married less than a year, and below them, on the first floor, lived a family of five. The two other flats, correspondingly below Mrs. Zaheer's, were vacant. Rosie would hear a few times each week the diligent young realtor showing them to prospective owners, the young woman's sprightly voice and foreign-educated English ringing in the stairwell along with the echo of footsteps and jangling keys.

When she first saw Mrs. Zaheer, Rosie judged her to be an arrogant woman from another time, full of class consciousness and prejudice. Rosie had kept her distance, until the day Mrs. Zaheer knocked on her door and asked her if she liked ginger tea. Since then, Rosie started visited her three, sometimes four, times a week; in the beginning she had felt awkward and guilty that she had been the one with the prejudices. As it turned out, Mrs. Zaheer was the opposite of arrogance, and all the prejudice inside her was accumulated as a result of a life lived, and not based on provincial values, which Rosie had to concede was the maker of her bias.

Rosie's proud father, the scion of a defunct feudal family, had framed portraits of his forebears hanging on the walls of his bedroom and living room. He would emphasize the importance of pedigree to Rosie, her two brothers and younger sister by pointing to them the portraits, naming each one, bowing his head at their feet with tears of reverence in his eyes. He had once beaten a man to within inches of his life for jumping over the boundary wall of the house to steal scrap metal that was set aside to be discarded during the construction of an additional garage. Despite every effort of the servants to shield Rosie and her sister from seeing the fiasco, Rosie had broken free, bolted through the kitchen, and out the back door, excited by the uproar in the middle of the night, just in time to see her father crash a metal pipe into the thief's ribcage. By that time her father had been using the metal pipe for long enough that it didn't matter to the thief anymore what he had jumped the wall to steal, or why he had made the decision to begin with, or why he had even been born.

The boy, Rosie remembered, could not have been more than fifteen. He was tied to one of the pillars of the second carport at the back of the house, bleeding from the nose and mouth. When he was untied, he doubled over like a deflated doll, his pulverized bones and flesh unable to hold him up.

Rosie had never told that story to anyone, not even Mr. Moyeen, because her husband had more affection for her father, Rosie felt, than her. Akbar Moyeen was the illegitimate son of a man who had died in poverty, and had left his real family and the one in which Akbar was born with little to their name. The Moyeen name came from Akbar's mother's side. He never knew his step-siblings. His single lament—from a man who never complained, and was annoyingly thankful and gracious throughout life—was not having the name of a father. He bore the Moyeen name with plenty of pride, and always paid it its due, stressing that it was his mother's bloodline to which he was thankful for having a name at all. So, when Rosie entered his life, and with her, her garrulous father with his ancestral pride and bearing that belonged to another age, with his handlebar mustache and fierce large eyes and a laugh that could be heard coming up the street a mile away, Akbar Moyeen quickly fell under his spell. He never mentioned it, never put words to the feeling, but Rosie became aware early on that her husband had adopted her father as his own too. Rosie didn't want to ruin the impression. She, instead, manufactured her own form of damage.

"Where is your mind today, my girl?" Mrs. Zaheer placed her large, thick-fingered hand over Rosie's, covering it entirely.

"Nothing," Rosie said absent-mindedly. "Nothing at all, Mrs. Zaheer."

"Sure," Mrs. Zaheer chuckled, and loudly slurped the last of her tea.

Rosie had been looking out the window. A bank of clouds was passing over the rooftops and lines of trees across their large backyard. The air was warm, carrying with it every so often the hint of rain. Rosie had wanted to plant a garden in one corner of the backyard, nothing elaborate: red roses, her mother's favorite, white roses, Rosie's favorite, sunflowers, and maybe some vegetables, cucumber, carrots. But she would have to clear it with the realtor and the other tenants and for that she had no patience. Mrs. Zaheer wouldn't object. The others, Rosie didn't know. The realtor, especially, she could do without, because the ever-chipper young woman would dole out a list of compliance issues and legal factors that would make no sense to Rosie, and leave her mad. The building was once owned by a family who lived on the first floor where they'd raised three children, sent them to study overseas, married them off, and after a few years the husband and wife died dignified deaths in the presence of their family and friends. Mr. Moyeen knew them. Rosie never developed an acquaintance.

"Now listen," Mrs. Zaheer patted Rosie's hand. "In all this talk of husbands, good or bad, we women forget everything else. Ourselves, our fathers, mothers, brothers, sisters."

Rosie had never heard Mrs. Zaheer speak of family other than her son.

"I got some news a few days back," said Mrs. Zaheer. "My sister, it's just the two of us left, and she's two years younger. She's sick, very sick."

"I'm sorry to hear that, Mrs. Zaheer."

"There was a time I could not go, wasn't permitted to go and be with my family no matter what happened. When my parents died, the bastard locked me up in the bedroom, and stayed up all night patrolling to make sure I would not find a way to go. My brother, when he died, my elder brother, the other one was sick in bed after a weeklong gambling binge, and I was stuck looking after him. Now my sister—if she doesn't live much longer, I want to be with her."

"That is very good, Mrs. Zaheer. You should be with her."

"Girl, your mind is in the stars and heavens," Mrs. Zaheer laughed. "Is it a man?"

"Who?" Rosie blushed.

"The way you're looking, what else can it be?"

"Mrs. Zaheer, no men have entered my life or thoughts since Mr. Moyeen—besides the vegetable and the chicken seller. Do they count?" Rosie laughed nervously.

Mrs. Zaheer seemed to take the joke with offense. Her face darkened, she pulled her hand away from Rosie's and stood. She took the empty cups and put them in the sink, ran the water, and wiped her hands on a small towel which had "Home Sweet Home" stitched on it. Rosie felt it was time to go and pushed back her chair. Before she could get to her feet, Mrs. Zaheer spoke again.

"I'm going in three days," she said. "To Chittagong. To be with my sister. My Kamran would have gone with me but he is out of the country, and won't be back unti—I don't know until when. His work schedule never makes sense. He has an office here, but he's never in it. Planes and airports have become his office. So. I will leave a key with you so you can water my plants for me."

She said the last part as though leaving instructions with a servant, then added: "I don't trust having that maid here when I'm not," she lowered her voice. "She's stolen from me with me right in the next room."

Rosie watched Mrs. Zaheer open an overhead cabinet and stretch to reach toward the back through a cluster of plastic bags of spices and condiments that crackled and swished as she moved them out of her way. She brought out a single silver key and set it on the table. "Just water my plants. No need to do anything else."

"Okay," Rosie took the key and closed it in her fist, like it was something precious to her that she had finally been handed down.

"I may be gone for a while," Mrs. Zaheer said, once more with the tone of addressing a servant. "If my sister dies, then—"

"I will pray for her," said Rosie.

"Don't waste your prayers, my girl. She's been ill most of her life. It's time for her to have peace."

On the day of Mrs. Zaheer's departure Rosie heard voices in the hallway at six in the morning, and looked through the peephole of her door. Mrs. Zaheer was giving instructions to a uniformed man in the same tone as she had directed Rosie to water her plants, and then the man lifted the two suitcases, which strained his narrow shoulders and pulled them down, and wobbled down the stairs. Rosie opened the door, and poked her head out. She was still in her nightgown.

"I was going to knock and see if you wanted tea before I left, but thought it was too early," said Mrs. Zaheer. "My flight leaves at eight-thirty. I hope this car service gets me to the airport on time. It's through my Kamran's work. He doesn't want his mother taking taxis. I don't tell him that I prefer rickshaws and scooters, and take them without his knowing all the time. Okay, my girl, just keep my plants watered." She went down the stairs without hurry. The world outside was waiting and would wait for as long as it took.

There were some half a dozen plants in Mrs. Zaheer's flat. Rosie watered them using a plastic container with a spout that smelled of disinfectant. She knew she was handling an object that was well cared for, and it made her feel as though her hands were soiled. All the plants were in the drawing room, half of them hanging along the bank of windows parallel to the ones in the kitchen and looking out over the backyard, and the rest arranged near the front door. After she was done, she washed the container, scrubbing it with the dishwashing soap, and then wondered if she'd made a blunder. Mrs. Zaheer probably had a special soap for it. Rosie left the container in the sink, and backed away from it like she'd just let go of a weapon she'd used to commit a crime.

She walked through the flat. Until now she had only been in the kitchen. Mrs. Zaheer had not invited her further inside, which was fine, because taking tea together in the kitchen made perfect sense. The walls of the drawing room were the same yellow-cream color as Rosie's, but there was wall-to-wall carpeting that was almost the same shade as the walls and as clean as if it had been laid minutes before.

Rosie stopped, walked back to the front door, took off her sandals, and resumed her tour. If she didn't know Mrs. Zaheer lived there, she would think it was a model flat the realtors had set aside for viewing purposes only. Nothing was touched, sat on, lived in. The sofa, matching loveseat, and a chair with an accompanying ottoman, had the fresh new smell of leather. The two table lamps on either side of the sofa had probably never been switched on. The coffee table was dust free. A mid-sized cabinet held a twenty-inch TV and a DVD player. Rosie wondered what kind of programs or films her neighbor watched. She had never heard sounds resembling either form of entertainment emanating from the apartment.

In the dining room was a table that seated a family of four. The table was a deep burgundy of expensive wood, maintained with as much care as the container for watering the plants, a tablecloth of brocaded patterns placed over it like a sheet over a corpse, never again to be lifted. At one end of the table was a china cabinet filled with dinnerware that had never been used, and never would be. Rosie cut through the dining room to the bedroom.

The four-poster bed stood a foot from the ground, with mosquito netting hung over and around it. The bed was made, the sheets drawn tightly, the surface of it as hard and smooth as a calm lake. The ceiling fan was on at a low setting, rotating with no effect over the still, damp air of the room. Rosie thought of turning it off, but changed her mind. Everything was deliberate, intentional. Mrs. Zaheer was not careless or tentative. If she left a fan on, she meant to do it. On the bedside table was the only picture in the flat.

A man about Rosie's age, and a woman, a few years younger, next to him, both forcing smiles for the camera, the woman seemingly more than the man. The man was a replica of Mrs. Zaheer, except for his build, which, Rosie could tell from the picture, was much smaller. It was as though Mrs. Zaheer's likeness had been fitted onto a body that was passing by, with the addition of a thin mustache. It was her son. Rosie thought that the bastard—Mrs. Zaheer's first husband, Rosie had to remind herself to say, instead of calling a dead man by an epithet she had no reason to use—must have been a small man, which made his abusive treatment of Mrs. Zaheer bizarre on top of horrible.

Rosie picked up the frame. On closer inspection, the man seemed to be carrying something heavy inside him, a weight that disallowed him from feeling what he wanted to at that moment and made him perhaps look smaller than he really was. The woman's forced smile was clearly annoying her. Rosie set down the frame. She looked at the smooth tabletop without a speck of dust and thought that Mrs. Zaheer would know that the picture frame had been moved from the way she had placed it. Rosie, thinking she had put it back where it had been, gave it a push to leave it slightly out of place.

Akbar Moyeen's presence as a partner had never been out of place. Even at the end of his long days with soldiers, at training sessions, briefings, countless meetings with superiors where the colonels and the generals loved nothing more than to condescend to young captains and majors, he would return home with a gift—flowers or chocolates or a dozen saris from which Rosie could pick what she liked or keep them all—and then sit with her, talking until they both began nodding off. In return Rosie was quiet, distant, unaffectionate. They did not make love on their wedding night.

A month passed before it happened. He made no mention of it during that time, left her alone, and when it happened, he was so gentle that Rosie didn't know they'd had intercourse when they were done. Instead of rolling off her, he rose to his knees, lay down on his back, and covered her up to her chin, like a precious artifact, and kissed her forehead. Rosie felt misused and wanted to slap him. And in the next instance, when he was asleep, his breathing as calm and undisturbed as a baby's, she was stricken with remorse.

She thought that when they found out she was unable to conceive, he would react. He did. But his reaction was gentler than if he had been comforting her after the death of a parent. He never mentioned anything about children again. One more count on which Rosie had stabbed him in the heart.

When she asked if he was happy, his answer was as uniform, consistent, and direct as had been his life—yes, he was happy, and he was thankful, he couldn't ask for more in one lifetime. He would add that he had seen too many men complain too often. Men who were angry and discontented no matter what fortunes visited them, and in turn made those around them miserable and immune to hope. There were people in the world who would never be satisfied. On a single day they could inherit more riches than could be of use in ten lifetimes, have perfect health, entitlement, freedom, mobility, and pleasures for the asking, and still they would wade through it all in search of one single, solitary fault. Not Mr. Moyeen, not Rosie's husband.

On a few occasions Rosie tested him. She tried to needle him into arguments, always starting playfully, and he caught on to their unserious nature, laughed, went with it, and treated her like a child. When she told him she was indeed serious, he sometimes crossed his arms and looked questioningly at her, as if he was looking at a stranger speaking a strange language whom he sincerely wanted to help. If only the stranger would act like what she was saying was important. All attempts were futile on Rosie's part. She had married a soldier who refused to fight.

He had fought. He had seen combat, and he had trained the young men who had joined the cause to liberate the country. In 1971, Akbar Moyeen was a second lieutenant. He had seen in action the great General Osmani who had turned fledgling bands of malnourished village boys into a guerrilla force. He had driven into the city with the liberation armies, quietly, listening, tired but alert. And then he had married. He remained a soldier, but his work and his dedication to the uniform stayed out on the fields and in his office. Other wives of officers would have traded in their husbands for an Akbar Moyeen any day of the week. They would have given up their ability to hear so as to not be forced into listening to one more word about discipline and duty.

Rosie knew. They had envied her, and Rosie did not miss the eyes staring at her husband, the stolen smiles, and the forced laughter at his inane humor, the murmurs that passed between the women like schoolgirls.

Nothing short of infidelity would stoke his ire. The enormity of the thought hit her later, and she wondered if murders got plotted the same way, with such ease.

The young man was Farzan Chowdhury, and he was the third and youngest son of an old Dhaka family that had made its name and fortune in the textile industry. A young officer—younger than her—Mr. Moyeen had been mentoring him after he received his commission into Mr. Moyeen's brigade. Rosie found it odd that the son of a rich man would go into the army of Bangladesh instead of the family business, but she soon learnt how much Farzan detested his father and brothers. His mother was his sole companion and confidante in the family. And soon, Mr. Moyeen filled the void left by the unwanted, demanding father.

Distance from the men in his family made Farzan comfortable in the company of women. From childhood, under his mother's constant watch and care, he spent most of his time with his aunts and his mother's friends. When he met Rosie, he told her, in the presence of Mr. Moyeen, his superior officer and mentor, that she should be written about in poems. Mr. Moyeen had laughed, and Rosie had found another odd thing about the young man. For who said such things in real life? She should be written about in poems? She could not stop the words from playing day and night inside her head.

Later, he told her he meant it. When Mr. Moyeen had gone to get an album of his graduation ceremony at Kakul Military Academy, Farzan Chowdhury had brought his face close to Rosie's and said if he could write that poem, he would. What Rosie naturally took as an advance was at first not. It was the only way Farzan knew to talk to women, because all his life they had come close to his face when they spoke to him, and his mother too when she talked to him about his life ahead, her dreams for him, transferred her words to his ears in whispers, quietly and confidentially enough to exclude the rest of the world. After that

Farzan had sat back and looked at Rosie until Mr. Moyeen returned.

Farzan began coming over for dinner, first once a week, and then up to three times, and sometimes on weekends. He joined the Moyeens on day trips to Savar, the zoo, Ahsan Manzil, lunch at old Dhaka. His respect for Mr. Moyeen was boundless. Mr. Moyeen spoke with him more freely than Rosie had seen him do with anyone else. Rosie even learned that, as a teenager, her husband had been in love. The girl he loved moved away, out of the country, and some years later he learned that she had gotten married. He had hoped they would come to be together but, recalling the story now, Mr. Moyeen laughed it off as youth's romantic hopes. Farzan, when he listened to Mr. Moyeen, or when they were engaged in conversation, was so completely tuned in to it that to Rosie he looked mesmerized.

The day that Farzan came full circle Rosie had returned from lunch and tea with a school friend who had moved to England and was on a short visit to Dhaka. He was waiting at the gate when Rosie stepped out of the car. He approached her and said hello. He held the door for her and apologized for being early. Rosie invited him in. She served tea and mentioned that Mr. Moyeen would be late. Farzan knew as much because he had less than an hour before been dismissed by his commanding officer. Yes, of course, Rosie admitted, how foolish of her. He produced a neatly folded sheet of notebook paper from the pocket of his blazer and set it on the coffee table, adding, "A very bad poem for a very good lady."

Rosie picked up the paper, held it without unfolding it, and they sat silently. Mr. Moyeen didn't come home until nine. The three of them had a late dinner, after which Mr. Moyeen spoke about the day with Farzan. Rosie sat with them and listened, and hoped the flush in her cheek and the thudding of her heart, and also that the scent of her on Farzan, didn't give them away.

There was worry in Mr. Moyeen's tone. Officers in the Bangladesh Rifles had been channeling reports to the army about discontent among soldiers in the organization, all of which the army had shrugged off, but could not any longer. Mr. Moyeen was a soldier first, an officer second, and his empathy and camaraderie were with his soldiers. Farzan listened to him with all the respect and reverence that had been in his demeanor throughout, like a son listening to his father's final words, but the entire time his eyes were on Rosie. Mr. Moyeen finished talking, a bit abruptly. His audience, he saw, was distracted. In that moment when he realized the cause of Farzan's distraction, Rosie was jolted out of her reverie and met her husband's eye.

Mr. Moyeen said he was tired and that Farzan should go home. Tomorrow was going to be long, as would the day after that, and the rest of the week. With things volatile at the BDR, which was now being taken seriously by the army, quite possibly for an indefinite time

"I like him more and more," Mr. Moyeen said, when Rosie came out of the bathroom, his eyes on Rosie. There was something animal in them, defiant and fearful at once, vulnerable and completely unbridled. "Don't you? I think if we had a daughter, he would be perfect for her."

Rosie sat at her dressing table and took the brush to her hair. In the mirror she saw her husband get up from the bed and come up behind her. He stopped her hand in mid-motion, took the brush, and picked up where she had been when he interrupted.

"More beautiful and ravishing than Rapunzel's," he said, running the brush through the thick curtain of Rosie's hair.

In the morning, when his alarm rang at five, for the first time since Rosie had met him, he said he was not feeling well. At first Rosie thought it was something minor. Exhaustion. Something he needed to sleep off. When he was still asleep at noon, Rosie's concern grew. She tried to wake him, but he groaned and waved her away, told her to keep the curtains drawn, leave him alone, and shut the bedroom door. When it happened that way again the next day and the day after that, Rosie knew something was wrong. She didn't need the unsatisfactory diagnosis to confirm that he had given up.

Mrs. Zaheer was gone a week when Rosie, alerted one night by sounds coming from her neighbor's flat, thought the place was being robbed. It was after ten P.M. Rosie was finished with dinner and watching TV. She never went out after eight in the evening, not even onto the stairwell, and the thought that she could be trapped in her apartment with burglars in the building made her feel as though a hand of ice had suddenly gripped her spine. She was afraid to call for the police. If the intruders next door heard her voice, they might try to break down her door, attack her. She wished one of the other neighbors would do something.

Frozen in her chair in the living room, Rosie turned off the TV, switched off the lamp, the kitchen light, the light in the bedroom, and stood blind in the middle of her home. Silly as she felt doing it, she began praying. Her mother came to mind; she'd had a habit of launching into prayers at the slightest provocation, no matter if the reason were genuine. Be it potentially worrisome news or a lost article of clothing—out would stream the three or four verses from the Quran she had memorized from her mother before her, and when the situation was normal again, attribute the end result to prayer and God. Rosie began whispering the verses from memory like she was conveying them to a confidante standing shoulder to shoulder with her.

Five minutes passed. Without moving her lips, Rosie prayed on, and then the sounds stopped. Immediately, she felt foolish. It was not because of her praying that the sounds had ceased. Unable to find satisfactory loot, the burglars had most likely abandoned the job. Or maybe they had found enough and left victorious. Rosie's mental inventory of Mrs. Zaheer's place did not produce anything of great value, but burglars were burglars, especially petty ones, like the poor soul that had jumped the wall of Rosie's childhood home. In that case Rosie would have to check on the place, tonight, or tomorrow latest, soon at any rate, before Mrs. Zaheer returned and thought Rosie had forgotten, as well as lost her mind, and not kept her word.

Then, through the silence, came measured, careful knocks. Rosie waited to gather her senses so she could understand if they were in fact knocks. She did not make a move toward the front door. The knocks sounded again. Three light raps at a time, as if the caller knew to be mindful that it was late. Rosie was about to ask who it was when it occurred to her that it could be one of the burglars; but that suspicion was soon upended by the reasoning that a burglar would not likely knock before entering. Looking through the peephole, she recognized him immediately: Mrs. Zaheer's son.

As she pulled open the door, the glare of the tube lights in the stairwell smacked her like a hand. Rosie blinked and squinted. When her eyes adjusted, she saw that he was grinning, having taken a a few cautious steps back from the force with which Rosie opened the door.

"I'm Kamran," Rosie heard him say. "My mother lives here. You're the neighbor I've heard so much about. Mrs. Moyeen, am I right?"

Rosie nodded vaguely, as if agreeing to an answer to a problem she didn't understand but did not want to give away her ignorance.

"Your mother is not at home," Rosie said. She felt foolish relaying a piece of information she figured a son would know. But a bigger concern sent her heart racing and face filling with heat. She was in her nightgown, braless, without any underwear at all, which suddenly made the glare of the stairwell lights ten times as strong. She slid further behind the door, a move that intensified the discomfort of the moment. Kamran, however, was nonplussed by the news of his mother's absence.

"Who knows what she's up to when?" he said, shrugging, the grin expanding.

"She says the same of you."

He grinned, said nothing.

"You didn't know she was going to Chittagong? To see her sister? Your aunt?"

Kamran's expression switched from light-hearted to surprised.

"Chittagong? Sister?" he said. "Ma?"

Rosie didn't know what to make of his reaction, until Kamran laughed and said, "Yes, I know. I was just joking to see what you would say. Sorry. Ma has talked a lot about you, and she's mentioned many times how serious you are." A pause of realization, and he said, "Oh my God! I'm such an idiot. Forgive me, please, Mrs. Moyeen, it's the middle of the night. You must think I'm a robber or something."

The only thing Rosie could think to say was, "Would you like some tea or something to eat?"

A childlike sheen fell over Kamran's face and he nodded enthusiastically: "If it wouldn't be too much trouble."

"Just give me ten minutes to get properly dressed," Rosie said.

Kamran ate like he hadn't had a meal in three days. He wolfed down every last morsel before taking a breath. He licked his fingers clean, chugged water, and then sat back like a happy emperor.

"Mrs. Moyeen, has my mother had this pleasure?"

Rosie shook her head, a silly blush heating her face. "Would you like something else?"

"There's more?" Kamran laughed. "I'll never leave your flat."

Rosie was ready to spoon more dal onto his plate, and her hand stopped in mid-motion. Seeing how little sense of humor she was able or prepared to entertain, Kamran said, "Sorry, Mrs. Moyeen. I have a big mouth. I should be saying thank you. So. Thank you. For this amazing meal."

"No. I mean, yes. It's no trouble. Your mother makes tea for me all the time."

"Oh, her ginger tea," Kamran laughed. "Yes. I think my stomach is permanently fortified against sickness. I've been drinking it since before I could walk or talk."

Rosie suddenly wanted to ask him a hundred questions. About his father, his stepfather, the bastard and the philanderer—it was, she knew, more than simple curiosity. She wanted to verify all that she'd heard. She could not place her finger on her reasons for it, but felt the unnamed grounds for having them pulsing inside her. Kamran seemed like the sort of person who would make for a poor fabricator. As a child he was likely the foil to every one of his mother's attempts at fibs. He was that little boy who would immediately pipe up about what he knew to be true and what facts he could hear his mother altering.

"Why so much regret in your eyes, Mrs. Moyeen?" Kamran's formality had suddenly dissolved. He leaned back in his chair, like a man who had returned home after a long time, picked a pack of Benson & Hedges from his breast pocket, and lit up a cigarette. "Ma spoke of you like you were a breath of fresh air and dose of sunshine all in one all the time. But you're not. Why so much regret?" He flicked ash onto his plate.

"Mrs. Zaheer and I speak of things that are not so serious," Rosie replied.

"My mother thinks seriousness is complaining incessantly about my father and stepfather. Anything else for her doesn't exist, or if it does, it pales in comparison to what she feels has been her plight in life. She's a good woman, Mrs. Moyeen, but wants to be seen as a martyr. All she ends up showing are her regrets. The same ones, over and over again."

Rosie felt heartened. Mrs. Zaheer's stories had some truth. The ex-husbands were real.

"Can I ask you something?" Rosie said.

Kamran nodded, smiled, and a dreamy glow took over his eyes. They were almost half-closed. He was handsome in a beaten way, Rosie thought. If that thief who had been nearly murdered by her father that night had somehow managed to live, he would probably have a similar look. Attractive, sullen, wise with a mixture of disaffection toward life as it was, as it came and went with its highs and lows and callous stabs.

"Was your father—did he beat her? Your mother said he did, all the time."

"No," Kamran smashed the cigarette in his plate. "He was a hard, rough man, but he never laid a finger on her.

He slapped me around a few times, but I was a reckless child. He yelled at Ma, abused her with names." Kamran watched Rosie with an expression after he was done that asked if she had more questions. "I'm sure she talked about the womanizing of my stepfather, too. Mrs. Moyeen, my mother's life stories are like a precious record collection. They will never change, and each time you hear one retold it will sound exactly like the last time, with all the inflections, digressions, and tonal shifts repeated.

"Yes, my mother's second husband was a man of many women," Kamran added. He was smoking again, and now Rosie found it offensive. His charm and suave presumptuous manner bothered her. She wanted to know what he was doing in the middle of the night bumping around next door, even if it was his mother's flat.

"Is that an appropriate way of putting it?"

Kamran stood up. His chair scraped. He began walking around, spreading his cigarette smoke around the flat like insecticide.

"How long have you lived here?" he asked. His tone was rigid, stern, like an inquisitor. Rosie wanted him out of her home.

"Long time," Rosie said.

"How long has Mr. Moyeen been dead?"

Rosie didn't answer. Kamran was in the center of the living room. The only light was coming from the hanging lamp over the dining table. In the spread of its dim glow Kamran was but a shadow whom Rosie would have shrieked at upon finding him standing in her living room in the middle of the night, even if she had known he was visiting but had momentarily forgotten.

"Many years," Rosie replied. "Your mother knows. Ask her if you don't believe me."

Kamran exhaled smoke, cleared his throat.

"What have you learned about me, Mrs. Moyeen?"

"Learned?" Rosie found it difficult to use the word in connection with something other than book learning, the kind she hadn't done since university. "Your mother said a few things, like most mothers, nothing too personal."

"And yet you're sitting there judging me, Mrs. Moyeen." His weight shifted.

"Judging you? Why would I do that? It's the middle of the night. I offered you food. What is there to judge for you or me?"

"You are a judgmental woman, Mrs. Moyeen. It's been in your eyes ever since you opened the door and saw me. Don't stand up. What have you done in life that's so good? That shouldn't be judged with the same eyes as you're judging me?"

Kamran's outline enlarged. He stopped a few inches from Rosie. Light from the hanging lamp over the dining table fell on his torso and arms, but his head remained in darkness.

"Have you ever asked forgiveness, Mrs. Moyeen?" Kamran's tone had softened, but kept a stern, manipulative edge. "Have you?"

"For what?"

"Mrs. Moyeen, it's a simple question. Have you ever asked for forgiveness? We're human. Any given moment of the day we're doing things that warrant asking for forgiveness."

"I don't do much. I stay home. I think of my husband, rest his soul. I eat, I sleep. What should I ask forgiveness for?"

"I've asked for it. Many times. Many times. Everyone deserves forgiveness. Everyone. Mrs. Moyeen. Down to the worst of the worst, even if they deserve nothing from us but spite."

"Did you get it?"

"It didn't matter, Mrs. Moyeen. I asked for it, looked to find it. That was enough."

"What do you know? About me?"

Kamran moved toward his chair and sat down. "It doesn't take much to know that you're burdened with guilt. But I don't judge you for it."

"Why would you judge me for my own guilt?"

"Because guilt is selfish. We think it makes us repentant, but that's not so. Guilt is us being selfish and wanting someone else to take our burden from us so we can feel good about ourselves. It has nothing to do with feeling good about someone else."

When he leaned forward, his expression chilled Rosie's spine. She was sure Mrs. Zaheer would've told her to expect a visit from him if that were the case. And she some-how knew that, despite what this man said, everything Mrs. Zaheer had told her about her life, and her husbands, was true.

She said, "Why are you in your mother's flat in the middle of the night?"

"She called me. My aunt died. Last night. Ma wanted me to pack some of her things and send them to her."

"I'm sorry. My condolences." Rosie felt the words come out of her like stones, things she needed to unload but wasn't sure how best to do it.

"I'll tell her, Mrs. Moyeen, thank you." Kamran's stubbed out his cigarette once more on his plate and stood, though she was certain he would never leave. He was here forever.

"Is there anything I can offer or send with you?" she asked woodenly.

"Mrs. Moyeen, you know how funerals are. My aunt couldn't swallow a glass of water without the pain making her cry in the end, Ma said, but there'll be people there gorging on food while mourning and praying for her soul to be forgiven and accepted into heaven."

And then he left without another word.

Rosie opened her eyes at the first light filtering through the windows opposite the bed, and bird chatter marking the passage of night into day. She sat up. She was still wearing the sari she had put on at Kamran's arrival. She opened the drawer of her nightstand and brought out the framed black and white picture and set it where it had been until recently. Mr. Moyeen, in uniform, angled away from the camera, three-quarter profiled, the beginning of a smirk around his mouth. In all those years Rosie had never noticed that. She used to tell him how serious he looked, and he said smiling in those official photos was forbidden, which was why he was doing all he could to keep himself from laughing. Imagining him laughing, Rosie thought about what he would have to say about forgiveness.

The Holdup

He swung. She struck. A cut opened over his eye. Her easily impressionable skin screamed out the bruises from his grip. A pain grew at the base of her neck from the force with which he shook her. The warm glow of the slap on her cheek wouldn't cool for two days. The children shrieked. Outside, the servants gathered, not surprised, pulled out of sleep that happened with one eye and one ear still open to the fight brewing since dinner.

Their daughter, Sana, called her aunt from the guest room phone, and an hour later Mitali's sister, Moina, was herding Sana and her brother Faisal into her car, while Moina's husband, Asad, spoke to Mitali and Hassan. He asked Mitali if she wanted to go with them and the children, and Hassan said she should. Mitali's rage reared up again. So he could spend the night with his whore, she yelled. Asad draped a hand around her shoulder and took her out into the hallway. Hassan checked the cut above his eye in Mitali's dressing table mirror.

"He won't go anywhere," Asad told Mitali.

"He will," Mitali fumed.

"Call him every half hour. Call him first thing in the morning. If he's not here, I'll scour the city for him with you. But this is not going to continue."

"Tell that to him," Mitali said.

"You're both responsible."

"No, Asad Bhai, no. Don't say that to me. You don't know anything."

"I've known you long enough, Mitali. I know you better than I know my own sister."

"No, you don't." She pushed past her brother-in-law and went toward the veranda to see the children. Inside the car Moina was speaking to them in whispers. Asad went back to the bedroom. He found Hassan seated at the edge of the bed, hunched over like a ruined man. Tiny drops of blood dotted the carpet between his bare feet.

"Sit up, the world isn't ending," Asad stood over Hassan. "When does it stop?"

"Bhai," Hassan couldn't stop a snicker from escaping, "after thirteen years, you want it to stop in one night."

In the next instance, Hassan felt a sudden gale rock him off his feet. Asad had his shirt collar in his grip and had yanked him off the bed. Asad was shorter than Hassan, but built like a small truck; he was a former cricket player and had been an amateur weightlifter during his university days. Hassan would have retaliated, pushed him, grabbed his wrist and shoved it back at him, but did not out of respect; Asad was ten years his senior.

"Your children, you idiot," Asad said.

"I'll die for them."

"Stop it," Asad let go of him, and Hassan sat back on the bed. "This stupid nonsense day after day, night after night. Die for them. What trashy movie do you think you're in? This is life. And listen to me: you'd better not leave this house."

"Ever again? Because that's what she wants from me—on-call, twenty-four-seven, shut inside this house. Is that reasonable?"

"Don't talk about reasonable. If you want to go to other women, then make a decision and end your family life."

"Asad Bhai, are you going to take the moral high ground with me? You're a saint, right?"

"No. I'm not a saint. But I did what I did long ago, long before you knew how to piss on your own. Moina knows, I know, our kids know. And those days are gone, behind me. Did I say you need to be a saint? Be a man. Figure it out, whatever that means to you both. You're not the only man working and taking care of a family. Grow up, for god's sake, and let us live in peace."

On the veranda, the servants were startled out of their silent enjoyment when Asad stormed out and shouted at them to go back inside.

"Imbeciles, every single one," he grumbled, getting into the front seat of the car. "What are you staring at?" he yelled at his driver. "Get in, do your job!"

"Don't shout," Moina urged. "The children are terrified."

Sana's mouth was clamped shut, her lips pulled in to keep them from betraying her. Next to her, Faisal's face was a teary mess. He was pushed up against Moina. Mitali was speaking to the children through the window, swabbing Faisal's face with the sleeve of her nightgown, reaching for Sana's hair to move it out of her eyes, which Sana was deliberately using for that purpose.

"Mitu, get in," said Moina.

"No. Just take them. Go be with your aunt and uncle for one night, okay? Have fun with your cousins."

"You should come with us too," said Moina.

"No."

"Let's go, then," Asad complained. "Already a scene has been created for the whole neighborhood, again. Maybe one of these days you people will understand you have a name to uphold."

The driver started the car. Sana was turned away completely from her mother's attempts at affection. Faisal's head was nestled between his aunt's pendulous breasts, hanging as they were bra-free inside her house-dress. Moina was three years older than Mitali. Since their childhood she had been more mother than an older sister to her younger sibling. To her niece and nephew she had been an older mother, a figure midway between aunt and grandmother.

Mitali moved away from the window, and the car began pulling out of the driveway. In the glare of the headlights, she was a washed-out apparition, a grim, unhappy ghost. Faisal's head popped out of the window. "Good night, Ammu!"

"Good night, my souls. See you tomorrow. Be good at Khalamoni and Khalu's, okay?"

Mitali slept the rest of the night in the guestroom with the door locked. It was past two o'clock when she lay down on the floor with a cushion under her head, and she was up again at five. She checked on Hassan in the bedroom. He was splayed across the bed the way he would be after a night-long drinking binge.

Hassan's affairs were not secret, or even discreet, despite his efforts to keep them covered up with deception and lies. Eyes and ears were everywhere, harvesting gossip fodder. Hassan and Mitali Qureshi were too good not to pounce upon. Second cousin to one of the country's richest industrial barons, Hassan's reputation, professional and personal, was no less conspicuous. He accused Mitali of being petty, like the vicious bitches and their catty jealousies that spread rumors about him because their sorry lives had no worthwhile purpose. They were not her friends, he reminded Mitali. Their husbands couldn't stand them, their children hated them, and they were consumed by self-loathing to boot; so the best way out was to use their snotty noses to poke into and stain other people's lives.

And then last week Mitali saw him at the roundabout in front of the Sheraton Hotel in the driver's seat with the woman (whom she had heard about and suspected he was screwing) on the passenger side. She had looked directly at him from the backseat of the car that was for her and the children's use, and he had looked away, casually, as if strangers' eyes had met in the middle of the city.

The woman was a former ingénue in films. No matter the caliber or quality of her films, for Mitali they were little better than dregs. She had not seen them. She didn't know the woman other than by name, which was Pinky Humayun in full, just Pinky in the papers. She knew that the woman was older than Hassan by at least fifteen years. Hassan, Mitali would say, was still grabbing for his mother's teat when that woman was making her rounds in the film industry, letting every greasy and lecherous hand that could push her career forward fondle her with impunity. She had returned from obscurity, much like a film star reviving a forgotten, once enviable career, through her affair with Hassan.

Mitali had asked the driver to confirm that what she was seeing was not a trick of her imagination. The driver, embarrassed, and caught by conspiracy of circumstance and timing in the middle of the domestic tiff he was very well aware of, kept his eyes on the road, looking for the first viable inch to make an escape. But Mitali insisted, and the driver had, reluctantly, to confirm that it was indeed Hassan in his car with the woman next to him. Hassan never looked back at Mitali. When traffic moved, so did their respective cars.

Hassan said she was the wife of a colleague and he was giving her a ride home. He made no acknowledgment of being acquainted with her in the past. But Mitali had a bone between her teeth. She growled, she clamped down harder. Hassan's first slap threw her off balance, but only long enough for her to gain the energy she needed to swipe back at his face. A nail tore the skin just above his eye, below the eyebrow, a precarious place that could not be reached with the greatest care without fear of hurting the eye. Mitali's anger made the clean cut with precision, and the blood trickled out. Hours would pass before the smarting of her own face would nudge her for attention.

He could hear her on the phone in the living room. The conversation seemed to last hours, her voice rising and falling naturally, unperturbed, as if engaged in the most banal exchange, before ending abruptly. It was her sister. Hassan didn't need to hear the conversation to know that Mitali had refused to accept certain facts Moina had tried to get her to see.

The pain over his eye was a pulsing reminder, an alarm to make sure he wouldn't grow complacent and forget about it. He should have iced it hours ago, put a Band-Aid on it. Now it burned when he blinked. He touched the crusted blood, which had leaked onto the bed sheet and turned a deep brownish red. By the time he was out of bed, he heard the car Mitali and the children used being started. He made it to the veranda, newly aware of a headache clamped around his skull like a helmet, as the car nosed out into the street and drove off.

Later, Hassan made a stop at Asad's office before going by their house to pick up his family. Asad was his usual stoic, unperturbed self. He was not happy to see his brother-in-law, and not just because it was during work hours. Asad had reached the conclusion that he did not like

Hassan. It was not a judgment on Hassan's philandering or his drinking. Asad had done enough of both to wreck his first marriage. Asad's qualms were with Hassan's handling of situations without regard to discretion. The repetitions made it worse, and the more Asad got pulled into the orbit of Hassan's perfidies the less he wanted to lay eyes on him again.

"Why don't you call before coming to my office?" said Asad.

"You wouldn't take my call if I did."

"Exactly. I'm not your father or your mother or your brother."

"I don't want to lose my children," said Hassan.

"Don't make me laugh."

"I swear I was going to tell Mitali about Pinky."

"You saved yourself some trouble, so there."

"I'm not like you."

"No one is like anyone else. Such stupid things! I can't sleep because of your domestic garbage every other night, and you're here trying to solicit my sympathy because you think, despite what you say, that we *are* alike. We are not. You have so many friends in this city, go get them involved in your mess. Stay or get a divorce. What more is there to think about?"

"It's not always true, Asad Bhai, what she starts fights about," said Hassan. "You got the better sister."

"Is that you being funny?"

"No. I'm just going to go and get them from your house."

"Wait." Asad stood and went around from behind his desk to shut the office door. "I'm your wife's sister's husband, but I won't think twice about setting you straight once and for all. I've known Mitali since she was a girl. Shape up, Hassan, or life will disappear around you one step at a time. You'll be standing in a desert before your prick can get hard for the next affair."

Hassan nodded, allowing Asad's seniority to rule.

"I know this actress," Asad said. "She's my age, probably older. I remember her films during the Pakistan time. Awful, dreadful films. No plot, no script, just excuses for her to show her midriff and shriek at villains trying to fondle and attack her. Her father was someone once upon a time. Her whole family was before she flushed their name down the toilet."

"You're being unfair," Hassan said.

"You aren't thinking with your head. Go. Get your wife and children and take them home."

Pinky Humayun had recently divorced her fourth husband and met Hassan at the Dhaka Club while there for the Club's election night fete as a guest of the newly elected president, who was a school friend of Hassan's. She had reverted to her maiden name, which had been the name she was known by at the start of her film career. Her father, with whom she had not spoken from the day she decided to work in films to the day he died, had been a civil servant, and so dropping the last name for her film image was a way of dissociating his connection to her chosen lifestyle and vice versa, as well as economizing on a grave sounding full name into the singular, upbeat Pinky.

From her fourth husband she had been smart enough to get the large house in Dhanmondi, one of the four that his family owned in the area. She lived there constantly in the family's crosshairs, forever sighted for destruction because of the pain she had caused her husband, who had been gracious enough to marry her in the first place, knowing her reputation and history. Of course, they didn't know of the nights and days he forced her down, held her legs open, and entered her with the back end of a long American made flashlight to see how much of it she could take. Once he tried it with a cricket bat after hitting her with it across the knees to disable her first. She had bled and shaken from the burning between her thighs for a week and did not go to the doctor. After the end of three marriages that left her repeatedly destitute, the fourth time around she had learned a few things and, in exchange for her torment, got something out of the divorce.

Hassan parked the car at the back of the house, entered through the kitchen, and crept up the stairs to the third floor. The first and second floors mostly remained unused, hollow and dark, full of lost echoes and swallowed light. Each time Hassan entered the house he couldn't help feeling stricken by melancholy, even if he was coming over for an afternoon tryst.

She was on the back veranda flipping through an old issue of an American movie magazine, sipping a cold drink out of a tall, narrow condensation-beaded glass, in her black silk dressing gown. Hassan had not seen her in anything else at home. Her hair was combed and hung down to the small of her back like a smooth, henna-tinted curtain. Three fans, hung along the ceiling at measured intervals, were all turned on. The small wicker table for three where Pinky was seated was set up at one end of the long veranda that looked down on the back lawn. A gardener was at work on the lawn's several flowerbeds. One corner of the lawn was in the shade of a Krishnachura tree full to bursting with red blooms.

Pinky didn't bother looking in his direction. "I hope this won't take long."

"How do you get to be the one that's mad? I had to go through everything while you sit here reading your lousy little magazines, dreaming."

"I live alone," was Pinky's reply. "I am alone. People I see on the streets are strangers to me. Even in this small city, even after my career. You, my dear, just have bad luck."

"I didn't come here to get mad."

"Don't stay if you're changing your mind about that. I'm very tired."

"From what?"

"My gardener down there is stronger than he looks. He's very protective of me. Stayed with me after my last divorce. He threatened my ex-husband once when he heard him yelling at me, and took a beating like a man."

Hassan came to the table and stood in front of her. Pinky's head remained downturned to her magazine. She was going from one page to the next as if speed-reading. Under the one she was reading was a small stack of other magazines.

"Don't lecture me," Hassan said. "She saw us that day in front of the Sheraton."

"Unfortunate, but good too, no?" She looked up. "You young couples fight like such children." Hassan had stuck a hurried Band-Aid over his eye, and it had come undone. The dried blood had scabbed over the cut.

"I don't want us to stop..."

"Stop what? Go be with your family."

"And then?"

Pinky dropped the magazine on the floor and began going through the stack. Some of them were very old and didn't have covers. Others had covers that were half-torn across the faces of the stars on them; sometimes it was the upper half of the face and sometimes the lower half.

"And then," she settled on a rare one, with its cover still entirely intact. Hassan recognized the actress on it as Meryl Streep. "And then," in one continuous motion Pinky tore off the cover, held it in front of her like a mirror, and placed it on the table. "And then, and then."

"I go through hell because of us and you can't say one word to my face?"

"Hell. Your pretty young wife opens a cut on your face and it's hell. You silly, ego-driven little man."

The gardener moved from one section of the lawn to another, sneaking a glance at the veranda on his way.

"Okay then, I'm going. Enjoy looking at your washed up movie stars whom you'll never be like."

A childish exit, Hassan thought, rushing back out, low and too derisive to have force. He passed the gardener as he cut across the lawn and went out the rear gate. His car, parked next to the gate and as close to the boundary wall of the house as possible, had become a point of curiosity and play for the neighborhood urchins. A half dozen of them were flocked around it, pressing their faces against the rolled up windows to get a better look inside. Hassan barked at them, and they crowded around him with palms up. He shooed them away, unlocked the car and climbed in. He had to startle and scatter them with the car horn before he could drive away.

Traffic was at a standstill on Satmasjid Road. Hassan had barely nosed into the stalled traffic, honking and cursing, being honked and cursed at, before sitting trapped.

Mitali should be asking for a divorce. He had no trouble thinking that, and it wasn't because he wanted it too, nor was it entirely altruistic on his part. The marriage was a mistake. He knew it, she knew it, they both knew the other knew it. It was fending off a seemingly bigger mistake that kept the divorce at bay, over concern for the children, when it was the only correct decision that could be made in a choice that had been too long overshadowed by premature notions of romance, and pride. Sana, would men be ruined for her? For Faisal, what would women signify other than mother?

Hassan rewound his thoughts, wishing they had never happened. Children were supposed to be better, stronger, and wiser than their parents, not only because of them, but because Nature's perseverance to better itself—instilled as that resolve was in so much of the human race—had to be a fundamental truth.

Forty minutes later he had moved less than two feet. To his right was Road No. 12A. Hassan could see down it through a gap that would not remain for long, and it was just wide enough for his car to turn and speed through. Pressing down on his horn, its high, nasal whine coiling out into the heat and the dust and the bodies, Hassan shifted into first gear and floored the gas. A young father holding his daughter by the hand screamed and, just in time, yanked his little girl out of Hassan's way. Hassan pulled over immediately. In his rearview mirror, he saw the man shaking his fist, cursing. He wanted to get out, apologize. But that would make matters worse. He gripped the steering wheel, leaned his head on it, and for a moment closed his eyes.

He was ready to drive again when the sharp jab bit into his shoulder. Hassan looked through his window, his head still reeling, at half a face. The eyes, under heavily sweating brows, were open wide, as if being forced to become so after endless sleepless hours. From the nose down, the face was covered with a filthy handkerchief that was once white. The hair on his head was greased into thin strips and badly parted down the middle. Hassan felt the sharp poke again, and saw the blade boring into his shoulder.

"Get out of the car," the voice spilled out from beneath the handkerchief, high and nervous, but steady.

"Don't try anything, sahib, just get out," said another voice, from the back. Hassan turned, but couldn't see him. The second was a voice that sounded like it had been shredded just minutes before with shouting.

"Didn't you hear me? Us?" The first one said, digging the blade into Hassan's shoulder. "What are you looking at? Get out of the car at once."

Hassan didn't think about it. He shook his head, cocked his right arm, made a fist, and flung it out the window. The blow caught the mugger on the nose. Hassan felt the cartilage against his knuckles, surprised at the force with which his fist had made contact. The nose pressed down like it was made of pliant rubber, nothing inside to resist or break. He saw, almost simultaneously in his rear-view mirror, the partner. While the first one howled and stumbled back and crashed to the ground like a felled tree, Hassan put the car into reverse and gave it gas. The second mugger shrieked just as the car was about to make contact, dropped something that clinked weakly on the ground, and ran.

Leaving the car running, Hassan stepped out. Within seconds, Hassan noticed the blade the second mugger had dropped lying on the ground like a dead fish.

"Oh mother!" the first mugger groaned, clutching his nose. Blood had soaked through the handkerchief, but he was still cognizant enough, or in too much pain and shock, not to have removed it. Hassan picked up the discarded blade. It was light and old, barely sharp enough to cut through a piece of paper, the damp wooden handle almost decayed and smelling of garlic.

"You wanted to rob me, is that it?" Hassan said, standing over the first mugger and kicking his hip.

"Oh mother! I beg you, sahib, don't! It was his idea."

"Who? That coward that left you here?"

"Oh mother! Oh my nose!"

"Shut up."

Hassan reached down, grabbed his shirt, which looked like the clean white shirt of a school uniform, and yanked him to his feet.

"Stop crying," Hassan told him, "or I will use this thing to cut off your nose altogether."

He reeked of old sweat and stale breath. Upon closer inspection Hassan saw behind the handkerchief the shape of a rounded jaw line, a face that had been plump with baby fat until recently, and eyes timid and squinty, which the boy had tried to make look large and threatening. Hassan stood almost a foot taller than him. At six-three, Hassan was taller than most Bengali men. The boy was a limp old rag in his clutch.

"I beg you, sahib, please, I just want to go home."

"Home? You cunning little idiot, you want to go home? You think this is a game?"

"Sahib, Allah is my witness," the boy whimpered, choked, his eyes red and fluttering, filling with tears, "I didn't want to. It was Malik's idea." He shot a glance in the direction Malik had escaped. "Please, sahib, I beg you, let me go."

Hassan pulled him around to the passenger side, and opened the door.

"You're going home," he said.

"Sahib, no, please."

"Shut your mouth and get inside."

Broken down and sobbing, the boy jostled into the passenger seat, and Hassan shut the door. A few heads briefly turned toward them. Rickshaws slowed as they passed. The boy looked out the window desperately to see if anyone out there would rescue him. He gasped when Hassan got in and slammed his door.

"Keep that blood from getting on my seats," he said. He put the car in gear.

"Where do you live?" he asked after a few minutes. When the boy didn't answer, he said, "You don't tell me, I'll take you someplace worse."

"It was Malik, sahib," the boy blubbered. A bubble formed at the corner of his mouth. He had taken the handkerchief off and was holding it, in a ball, against his nose.

"That doesn't mean you are not also responsible. Who is Malik to you?"

"My...my...he is my..."

"Stop blubbering like an idiot and answer properly."

"My cousin, sahib."

"He's a bigger idiot than you. And a coward. And what's your name?"

"Kalam, sahib."

"Stop calling me sahib. Where do you live?"

"I beg you, sahib...I mean...sorry...please, I beg you, just let me go."

"Only way you're going home today is this way. Up to you."

Kalam led them to the Malibagh Bazaar railway crossing, and told Hassan to stop the car just past the tracks.

"Which one?" Hassan asked.

Kalam gave him a look as if he'd just woken up and discovered he was in a stranger's car. On the opposite side of the road, traffic was piling up as the arm began descending for an oncoming train. A half dozen rickshaws and as many scooters scrambled to beat the jam, irritating the drivers of cars they cut off in the process. Horns shrieked in a range of notes. One driver rolled down his window and told the rickshaw pullers to go fuck nine generations of their forefathers.

"I'm telling you again, you show me where you live, or I take you somewhere worse," Hassan said, heightening the seriousness of his words by cutting the engine. "Your decision."

Without thinking about it Kalam brought down the handkerchief. The blood was smeared and dried over his mouth, and part of his nose. He would be sore for a few days, but it wasn't broken.

"Throw that disgusting thing away," Hassan told him. Kalam's eyes narrowed. He looked longingly at the handkerchief before balling it up more than it already was and flinging it out the window. His arms were thin and bony. His neck sat like a pencil on his shoulders. On a slim and weak-looking torso, he had a paunch that had accumulated thirty years too early. He clamped his hands together over his stomach, and Hassan thought he was going to implore and beg and cry again.

"That one," Kalam pointed at a dingy gray building next to the line of shops they were parked by.

"Okay," said Hassan.

Kalam opened the door and hurried out. Hassan was just as fast and cut him off around the front of the car.

"Not so easily," said Hassan. When he reached again for Kalam's collar, the boy yelped and blocked his face with his forearms. Hassan took the collar in a firm grip without choking him and pushed him forward.

"Wait." Hassan stopped in front of the first open storefront. A shriveled old man was sitting behind a counter selling beedis, matches, incense sticks, miniature vials of attar of rose, and bottles of coconut oil. Hassan reached for his wallet with his free hand, but unable to get his money out, freed Kalam's collar.

"Don't think about running." He took out a fifty-taka note, while Kalam stared hungrily at the wallet like it was food. "Here. Don't look so stupefied, it's not for you. Give it to him." Kalam looked from Hassan to the old storeowner, befuddled. He took the money from Hassan with a trembling hand, and walked it over to the store. "Chacha, look after my car for a few minutes," Hassan called to the store-owner. "And remember this boy's face." The store-owner nodded like he was expecting the visit, the money, and the instruction to remember Kalam. He didn't reach for the money, and Kalam set it down on the counter.

They turned left down a passageway between Kalam's building and the one before it. As soon as they entered the passageway there was the stench of sewage. The path was wet and littered with soggy pieces of newspaper, a child's sandal, discarded candy wrappers. In many places, it was stained red with paan and betel nut spit. Hassan covered his mouth and nose, his stomach tightening and gag reflex bucking.

Kalam stopped at a door nearly at the end of the building. A padlock hung on the bolt, undone. It was rusty and looked like a giant bug clinging to the last remnants of life. Kalam grabbed it and pulled it off the bolt. The door opened with a screech of the hinges. Kalam looked hesitantly at Hassan, hoping perhaps that he had seen enough not to want to go further, but Hassan, with his hand still held up to defend against the stench, waited to be invited in.

They went up a dank, slippery stairwell to the third floor. Hassan felt his footing slip a few times but feared touching the rusted railing more than falling. Kalam trotted up the stairs with the confidence of habit, as if the steps would never betray him. He knocked lightly on a door scarred with nicks and cuts. Above the door was a small framed picture of the Kaaba at night, in color, gleaming with lights shining from the surrounding minarets. Pilgrims in mid-motion were caught by the camera's eye as a moving white blur.

The door opened slowly, revealing a woman's face wrapped by her sari. She squinted exactly as Kalam did, and, recognizing the boy, opened the door wider. Seeing Hassan, she clutched her hand to her chest.

"Allah, what has he done now?" she moaned weakly. "What happened to your face? Allah, Allah, Allah, you will ruin us and send your father to an early grave."

Her bony arm jutted out of the darkness of the flat and grabbed Kalam's ear. Kalam winced without making a sound and got pulled inside.

"Go clean yourself," the woman said, straining to keep her voice low. "Allah, give this boy some...give us...give me..." Out of breath and limp with rage, she looked back at Hassan. "Come inside."

The raw odors of the stairwell and the vileness outside were replaced by those of stale cooking, old oilcloth, and coconut oil from the woman's hair. Hassan stood back in the hallway until the woman turned back around.

"Come in, please. I don't know what more to do with him," she said.

The sound of water splashing came from the other end of the small flat. Hassan followed the woman into a sitting area no larger than the hallway. A doorway led out of it toward a room on one end, and Hassan saw the glow of the morning filtering mutely through it and spilling into the sitting area.

"Who is it?" a feeble, broken voice called from the room. "Mother, who is it?"

The woman went to the door. "Don't get upset, Father."

"Oh, what has that good-for-nothing done now to rain shame on us?" The man's voice caught, and a sob escaped. Hassan sensed movement behind him, and turned to see Kalam there, damp-faced, standing in a defiant pose with his arms crossed. His nose was swollen. Hassan's knuckles tingled. Sympathy pain.

The woman sprang from the door of the inner room, past Hassan, to Kalam. She slapped him three times across the face. Kalam took the slaps and held his ground. His mother seemed oblivious to his nose.

"He is in there dying because of you, you louse," she said. "What have you done now?" She turned to Hassan. "Whatever he has done. Take him. Punish him in whatever way you like. He deserves it. Give him to the police and let him rot in jail."

"Mother, who are you talking to?" a terrible coughing fit followed. At the end of it the man drew in a long, painful breath, hacked, and spat.

The train whistle screeched, followed by the lazy chug and swish of it passing by, while around it horns blared and bellowed in the traffic backed up at the railway crossing.

"You scourge, you shame," the woman whimpered, unable to look at her son.

Hassan made his way toward the door.

"Have a cup of tea before you go," the woman called after him.

"Ma, who is it, for God's sake!"

"No one," she answered, without losing composure despite the anger and tears.

Hassan said nothing and pulled at the door, which stuck at first, then flung open like it was made of cardboard. Outside, he clipped down the fetid passageway, holding his breath. The store-owner watched Hassan as he walked by, and Hassan didn't give the man another thought until he reached his car.

"One tea with milk," Hassan said, walking back up to the store-owner.

"What's that boy done now?" the old man asked. He chuckled. He had no upper front teeth and missing ones on the bottom. "His poor father. Just lying there, waiting to die. All because of that boy."

Hassan finished the tea, and gave the man a little extra, but he didn't return to his car. Instead, he turned to look at Kalu's building, transfixed as if he was no longer inside his body. Then he began walking back towards the house.

The Forced Witness

Over the V created by two shoulders just below his eye level, Noor Muhammad could see the hole in the bay window, a jagged, yawning O, and the three constables who were stooped over the shards of glass on the pavement below the window ledge like pecking roosters. A thick-necked inspector, tapping his nightstick against his leg, was maintaining a stance of constant intimidation without needing to as he interrogated the servants—four men lined up in a single row. Noor, along with the other gawkers, all servants from surrounding homes, stood outside the main gate that had been opened all the way to accommodate the police jeep parked halfway into the driveway.

Fourth one in a week. The police wanted to write them off as acts of vandalism, chalking them up to the fact that a spate of American and British families with teenagers had recently moved into the area. But when valuables worth thousands were found lifted out of living rooms and bedrooms, official notions began to change. By the standards of the Gulshan district, it was a crime wave. Two on this street, where Noor Muhammad stood with the crowds outside his neighbor's gate; one on the next street over, and another—the first one—on the street closest to Airport Road. Coincidentally, the first one had occurred at the house next door to one of the foreign families, and for that reason alone had originally stoked police suspicion toward the kids.

Now the servants were shaking in their boots, and not just because it was a cool December afternoon with the sun barely filtering through an arrangement of ashen clouds, stretching to the limits of Noor's vision. He could sense the trembling of their limbs, the unsupportive emptiness in their stomachs.

The constables, unable to gather any useful information from the shattered glass, went to the inspector, and a quick conference followed. The inspector returned to the servants and lectured them further, their heads moving up and down obediently. Then they were dismissed. The inspector and his constables rushed back to the police jeep, and the inspector, before he climbed in, pointed his nightstick toward the crowd and said, "Get lost!"

The jeep growled awake, the tires streaked the pavement, as the constable at the wheel put the jeep in reverse, and with another shriek of rubber and friction, shot down the narrow street blasting exhaust fumes.

Someone snorted, "What in God's name will locking windows and doors do when they break everything in their way?" The neighbors' night guard, a rangy old soul named Rasool, dispersed the crowd. Only Noor remained.

"Of course the police think one of us did it," Rasool walked over, lighting a beedi, and speaking as if resuming a conversation that had been interrupted. "What else could explain a burglary in a house full of people? But these thieves, they're good. Not those oiled up urchins who pilfer the scraps we throw out. These crooks know what they're doing and do it well. They can steal your soul right from inside you and you won't know it's missing till the next morning."

"What did they take?" Noor asked.

"Television from the guest room," Rasool replied. "And a clock radio. It's that time of year. They know people will be away on holidays, and only us left. Best time to go on a rampage." He dragged the last of the beedi into his lungs, exhaled the acrid smoke in much the same way the police jeep had belched fumes from its exhaust, and crushed the tiny remainder of it between forefinger and thumb.

"Rain, it looks like," he checked the sky. The skin on his neck hung loose and creased, flecked with white stubble. "Maybe not. There's the sun breaking through over there." He lit another beedi. "These people are fools, but not thieves."

It took Noor a moment to understand that Rasool had been referring to the servants in his own house.

"These houses," he blew smoke through the perfect circles of his nostrils, "you can be in the next room and hear nothing, because the next room is a mile down the hall. And from the servants' kitchen in the back, we might as well be in a different city. The thieves these days, they're no fools. They just look for the best time, and they don't care if there are people in the house. Why else would they pick this neighborhood, these houses? Because they know the loot will be worth the trouble. That's how good they are. And the police? Biggest of all fools. Scaring the little servants is all they can do, because they know the thieves are a hundred times more clever than them."

"Keep your head clear, and your eyes and ears open," he told Noor. "That's the only thing these idiot policemen are right about."

Up in his room in the servants' quarters, Noor watched the last of a smattering of clouds drift apart. From behind the shadows appeared the late evening sun, a fiery lantern over the horizon that cast his room in an orange glow. Birds were shrieking themselves to sleep, and somewhere, not too far away, a trio of crows was in a cawing feud. Noor felt the chill air on his face from a passing breeze that made leaves hiss and branches scratch against each other and picked up in its stream the freshness of the lime trees.

Below his window the nightly card game was being played. The hushed chatter of the driver, the night guard, and the gardener could be heard, their laughter intermittently chopping through the air, and the scattered eruptions of jeering and whistles marking the end of one hand and the beginning of the next. In this manner it would go on for hours, long after Noor went to sleep.

The cold grew as the sun dipped. Noor heard the card players arguing whether to take the game indoors. He went out onto the balcony. "I'll make tea," he said. "Are you coming in?"

"Aha! You speak like God from heaven," the driver said. "Yes, we're coming in. Today I finally have these two where I want them and I'm not letting go. Make the tea good and strong, Uncle. These two will pay back every pie they ever made off me."

Laughter rose, challenges of fights to the death, and profanity. The men swept up their game and hustled it up the stairs of the servants' quarters to the driver's room. They shuffled past Noor—who was the eldest and received a modicum of respect for that—trailing cigarette and beedi smoke that made his eyes water.

Still thinking about the burglary next door, he went downstairs to the kitchen. He lifted the kettle off the stove, rinsed out the tea leaves from the morning's brew, and stood holding it under the tap, the water thrumming against the copper bottom at first and then gurgling up to the brim. As soon as he shut off the tap, Noor heard a noise—a clatter of something falling in the dining room—and grew still. His shoulders hunched and tensed. Motionless at the sink, the kettle clutched in his grip, he held his breath, listening for a repeat. A minute passed. Every sound came from the outdoors: the birds chattering in the last light of day, the winner among the trio of crows sounding its lone victorious caw. Noor shook his head, and glanced around the kitchen, as though it were full of people who could have witnessed his paranoia.

He sweetened the tea with condensed milk, poured out three cups, and covered the kettle with a tea-cozy. He laid out a pack of Nabisco biscuits on a plate, placed everything on a tray, and made his way back out and up the stairs of the servants' quarters. Night winds were forming, with steelier blasts of cold.

Approaching their door Noor heard a squabbling match in progress. Seeing Noor, the gardener shot up from his chair, as though the very person he was in need of to corroborate his point had at last appeared. The gardener was the eldest after Noor, with the night guard following, and the driver last.

"Two boys ganging up on one old man," said the gardener, wide-eyed, his gray beard trembling. "Insolent bastards. I have bad eyes, God help me. We'll see how smart they are when their's go to shit."

"Nobody is ganging up on you, Hashem Mia," said the driver. "Just take more time and look at your cards before making a call. Who's in a rush here? Relax and sit back down. Look, here's Uncle with tea."

"Don't you tell me to sit, boy," said Hashem Mia. "I'm taking a piss."

He stalked past Noor, out the door, pattering barefoot along the balcony and down the steps.

"Last three rounds he lost," said the driver, carefully sweeping aside their pot of money to make space for Noor to set down the tray. "Tea *and* biscuits, Uncle?"

"Just keep your voices down," said Noor, laying out the plate of biscuits, serving the cups of tea, and placing the tea-cozy covered kettle in the center. "This cold gives me headaches, and I feel one on the way. I'm going to keep warm and lie down in my room. There's plenty more tea in this." He gave the tea-cozy a pat, and set down the empty tray on the bed.

Making his way to his room, Noor saw Hashem Mia appear at the top of the stairs with a strange expression, as though he had suddenly forgotten where he was or where he was headed. Seeing Noor, his face stretched into a smile, and with a flash of recollection he sped up his steps.

"I'll show those boys who's an old man," he said, passing Noor.

He stumbled upon a dark room in a place that was at once familiar and strange. There was a sense of peril that made the nape of his neck prickly with the hair standing on end. He had heard a noise. It could have been something breaking or falling, a piece of expensive chinaware perhaps, a vase, but it was not. It was, very specifically, the deliberate breaking of glass. Blindly he walked along, as an unseen force propelled him in the direction of the noise.

Each step was slow and tentative, as he extended his arms out without finding a wall to guide him. Hours seemed to pass in blinks as Noor put one foot in front of the other, until his gait became fluid and steady, finally acclimated to the strange darkness.

But there was nothing. Only the sound of his voice, in conversation with itself, whittled down slowly, irreversibly by old age and impatience. He wished the bastard would just appear, descend from the darkness like a bird of prey with wings beating and sweep it all away. Suddenly his breath was plugged up, his legs scrambling to fight, spasms in his stomach. He could still inhale in spurts, feel the paranoid pumping of his heart in his brain, knocking in his chest, but exhaling became a struggle.

Then a flash. And a sudden release, like the blast of a trumpet—the desperation in his own scream sounding like the faraway din of someone else being dragged to their death. His shoulders were shaking, and he knew, finally, that he'd once had wings but they'd been clipped, leaving only the sensation of something in their place, a heightened presence and pain that would never leave him.

"Bad dreams?"

Noor's eyes opened to the grinning face of the driver.

"You were shouting," said the driver.

Disoriented, Noor gazed around his room, struggling to uncoil himself from the dream.

"What is it, Uncle?" the driver said. "What are you looking for?"

"I thought," Noor shook his head, "you know how it is when you have a dream that makes the real world look fake."

"Uncle," the driver chuckled, "I wish I could dream like that day and night. Even when I'm awake. Come. Come with us."

"No cards for me, I told you a thousand times."

"Some good cold air to clean out the bad dreams."

"I will take a thousand bad dreams over a cold. But has Hashem Mia calmed down?"

"You know how he is. Forgot anything had happened as soon as he came back from taking a piss. Like a child. Not the first time it's happened. He gets upset, yells at me and Abdul like we're his children or something, goes off for a piss, and comes back a different man. Poor fellow. Doesn't realize we never actually take his money. He forgets that we make sure he leaves with as much as he brings to the game."

"Worse than death is the demise into old age."

"It's not that bad, Uncle. We're going out to get some." The driver tilted his head back and mocked a swig. "Come with us."

"You go out in this cold all you want, I'm just fine here," Noor clasped his blanket around his shoulders.

"One little nip of the good stuff, Uncle, and you'll be warmer than a woman's embrace," the driver winked. "If you want, we can arrange that too."

"Drink and women at my age. My heart will stop just thinking about those things."

"You've done all there is to do, Uncle," the driver smirked. "I know without you telling me."

After they left, Noor went down to the main house, prepared a light supper, and ate it sitting on the small veranda behind the kitchen.

The night was clear. A half moon was wedged into a jagged shelf of cloud, and despite the glow from the streetlamps, the twinkling of stars could be made out in the sky. Noor remembered the pitch-dark nights in the village of his childhood, when full moons were the brightest (and only) source of light, and the intuitive knowledge the villagers had of the land that allowed them to go back and forth, in the blinding black, simply by the contours of the terrain under their feet, and by the lifelong comfort of memory.

He washed his plate, drank a glass of water, and turned off the kitchen lights, realizing that he did not feel at all well. He would return to bed and try to sleep it off. As he was making his way back out the rear veranda toward the servants' quarters, he felt his foot land on the clammy back of a cockroach. The tickle of its sudden desperation to live, before his weight exploded its plump guts, pushed him off his balance.

There were flashes then, orange and yellow, purple and blue, popping and winking through a swirling darkness as Noor discovered that he was falling.

A voice reached him from far, very far—a voice that was trying to penetrate a membranous filter that was devouring it before it reached his ears. He was being jostled, his consciousness throbbing at the back of his skull. Shapes emerged around his vision, first as stark outlines against the light, and then filling in to reveal their human forms.

"Uncle? What happened?"

"Noor Muhammad?"

"Noor?"

"Is he dead?"

"*Oho!* Hashem Mia, sometimes it seems like it's your entire mind that's fading along with your damn vision. The man is clearly breathing."

"Boy, don't test my temper, I'm warning you."

"Both of you, stop."

"What's this under his foot?"

"Poor fool must have stepped on it in the dark."

"He's fine. Abdul, go call the police."

Footsteps trotted away.

Noor felt water on his face, in sprinkles, cool and sudden, as the conversation crystallized. The driver was leaning into his face, shaking him by the shoulders, repeating, "Uncle? What happened?"

Hashem Mia lowered himself on his haunches on the other side of Noor, peering down at the cook's face like a doctor concentrating on the first move of an intricate procedure.

"Uncle, did you fall?" the driver asked.

"I stepped on something—I think," Noor managed.

"That you did," said the driver. "A big, fat son of a bitch of a cockroach. The thing burst open like a jar of cream."

"Hold this against your head," said the driver, placing a plastic bag filled with ice in Noor's hand. "There's a nasty bump on the back."

It was just below his bald spot, a protrusion as round as a small coin, tightly plump with blood and pumping pain to the beats of his heart. Touching it made him gasp.

The door between the kitchen and the dining room swung open, and Abdul returned, slightly out of breath.

"The police will be here," he said. "Maybe in an hour."

"Maybe never," the driver said. "Let's take him up to his bed."

"Police? Why police?" Noor hadn't registered this before. Now he tensed up.

"Uncle, you stay calm for a moment," said the driver.

Noor felt his own weightlessness when the driver and the night guard lifted him by his shoulders and ankles. The trip out of the kitchen, up the stairs of the servants' quarters and into his room felt like being on a rocking boat. Hashem Mia followed carrying the bag of ice, which he handed back to Noor once he was laid down.

"Uncle, do you remember what happened?" the driver asked. A different seriousness had fallen over his tone, one that went deeper than simple concern for Noor.

"But why the police?" Noor insisted.

"Noor Muhammad, stop being a stubborn old goat," Hashem Mia groused.

Noor blinked at the gardener, and said to the driver, "I ate dinner. Then I cleaned up. I was coming up to bed when I fell. Next thing I know everything went dark."

The driver let out a long breath. "You didn't hear anything then?"

"Next thing I heard," Noor replied, "was your voice."

"You heard nothing else?" said the driver.

"How could I hear anything in my condition?" said Noor, making an effort to sit up, and dropping the bag of ice on the bed.

"Uncle, keep it on your head," said the driver, picking it up and pressing it in Noor's hand.

"When my head hit the ground it was like someone had bashed it with a metal pot," said Noor. "I'm lucky to be alive."

"Looks like your head landed on the mat by the dining room door," said Abdul. "Lucky for you it happened like that."

"Did you hear anything break?" the driver asked.

"Yes," Noor snapped, weakly, "the sound of my own head splitting."

"The glass of the front door was broken," Abdul said. "The whole panel. They took the stereo from the living room and the two big crystal vases off the dining table. And you heard nothing? Any other time we can't whisper without your ears pricking up, and now you say you didn't hear the sound of a sheet of glass being shattered? You expect us to believe that?"

"Abdul," the driver held up a palm. "Get out of here. Go. Have a cigarette. Calm down."

"Don't tell me to calm down, Rahim," Abdul snapped. "I'm going to lose my job for some old fool who doesn't know to look where he's stepping? He's older, but we're all the same here. The house is our equal responsibility. When it rains shit on one of us, it rains shit on us all."

"I'm an old man, you bastard," Noor Muhammad rose to a sitting position. "I made my dinner, did my work, and I was coming to bed. You people were up running through the streets when you should have been here. You're the night guard," he pointed at Abdul. "Where the hell were you?"

"If I lose my job, old man," Abdul seethed, "I will find you in your worst dreams and pluck out the hairs of your beard one at a time, for every taka that I lose." He stalked out. Noor, Rahim, and Hashem Mia heard a string of profanity and Abdul's footsteps rapidly fading as he marched toward the stairs.

The banging was rapid, impatient. One after another, swift, blasts against the metal gates out front, and echoing up and down the driveway, all the way up to Noor's room, jostling him out of sleep. A pulsing headache sent tremors from the bump on the back of his head to his temples.

Noor heard footsteps rush past his door. He knew they were those of one of the other three men, but unsure which as their tense whispers muddled together. "Hurry, hurry, they're here." The pain in his head was momentarily subdued by a surge of adrenaline that sent his heart racing. He lifted his heavy head off the pillow, peeled off the blanket around him, and swung his legs off the bed. His knee buckled as soon as he stood up; immediately he felt the full force of his headache return.

He doubled over. The ground swirled as the inside of his head rotated like a carousel, and from the front of the house came the grunting approach of a vehicle. Noor straightened slowly until he was able to stand again without swaying. He felt the need to tiptoe to his door—why is it that the mention of the police, let alone their presence, turns people with nothing to hide or worry about into edgy, crouching trolls?—and cocked an ear to the world below.

Multiple conversations and half-finished phrases floated up, consistently urgent. Noor could make out Rahim taking the lead, Abdul corroborating as needed, and Noor imagined Hashem Mia standing there, mute—as he sometimes did for hours, staring at a flowerbed or newly manicured section of lawn.

"Bring the *laad*-sahib down!"

It was the first full phrase Noor heard clearly, and once more his heart raced perilously.

Noor was at the top of the stairs when he saw Hashem Mia bounding up the steps. When their eyes met, the gardener had the expression of a reluctant assassin.

"Go," said Noor. "I'm right behind you."

"Hey asshole, are you too good to come down like the rest of the household?"

It was the inspector Noor had seen next door, standing with one fist dug into his side, and his nightstick tapping against a leg. Hashem Mia cast a glance at Noor over his shoulder, his eyes stricken with fear. In his rush Noor forgot his sandals, and the wet grass of the rear lawn sent shivers through his body. When he reached the driveway, the pavement was a slab of ice.

"Get over here!" the inspector growled. Like the grunts of the jeep that brought him here, the inspector's roar hung over the driveway before fading into the unaffected chirping of crickets.

"My honor," the inspector stepped toward Noor. To Noor's right were Rahim and Abdul, heads bowed, arms clasped against their abdomens, in identical poses as though in prayer, and behind him Noor could feel Hashem Mia lingering. "Have we rested well? Got enough sleep? Taken our sweet time fucking off while thieves take over the house?"

On his breath Noor smelled the mixed odors of betel nut and endless cups of stale tea. The man loomed over Noor so completely that the inspector's height and frame fully obstructed his view of the diminutive cook behind him.

"Why did you make me wait, asshole?" the question leaked out of the inspector's mouth like slow poison. "Do I look like your bitch mother or whore wife?"

"Sir, he was ill," the driver began, before the inspector's hand flew up from his side like an elephant's trunk and thrashed him across the face.

"You were telling me," the inspector returned to Noor. The headache, now in Noor's temples, felt like two nails being hammered into his skull. "Why did I have to wait out here in the cold and call you and call you before you took the trouble to come down? What's up in that room you're hiding? Oh, you don't have to tell me. I'll find out."

His two constables, attuned to their boss' methods and inflections, began jogging toward the servants' quarters, the rifles slung over their shoulders swaying from side to side.

"Don't think because you're a little old man that I won't put this stick up your ass to make you shit the truth," said the inspector. "I've seen feeble-looking bastards like you rape little girls, and I've smashed in their balls. How convenient, right? He was ill and sleeping. The only one in the whole house right when there's a burglary. It's always sleep."

"Sir," one of the constables said when they'd both returned from ransacking Noor's room. "Nothing but this tin with money. About five thousand takas." Noor's savings over the last two years.

"Even I don't have that much money at my house," the inspector smirked. "You're mine, old man. Take him."

"Sir, please," the driver spoke again, and a slap to the face once more cut him off. The two constables grabbed Noor, one of them flinging the blanket off his shoulders to the ground. His feet lifted from the ground a couple inches as the constables herded him by his armpits to the back of the jeep.

The dank wetness of the cell crawled up Noor's nostrils. His wrists were shackled and tied over his head by a rope to a ceiling fan hook. He was seated on the ground, his legs stretched out before him, a pinprick of pain forming at the small of his back.

"This asshole sleeps more than my daughter's goddamn cat," a voice boomed in the hollow room. Noor, demented with pain, still recognized the inspector's bass. A jolt hit the balls of his feet. His throat, prickly and hoarse from hours of being torn with screams, was again set on fire. "It's time to have our chat, asshole."

Two more strikes to the soles of his feet, and Noor felt his eyelids drooping and the world once more dissipating. He could only clench his teeth and groan rather than articulate a scream.

A chair clattered next to him, and the weight of the inspector took it over. Noor's head got pulled to the side by his beard. As the inspector dragged his face from side to side by his beard, Noor felt no new pain.

"How many of them are there?" the inspector said. "Is it a gang? Talk, shit-eater. Is it? Are you the innocent-looking leader? How many of you? I'll hunt down every one of them and string them up by their balls. How many? Where? Are you a Hindu kaffir? You will die here and be buried under this floor, so you can hear my voice for the rest of eternity."

"On my mother's soul, my lord, I know nothing," Noor sputtered. The words scratched their way out of his throat.

The inspector released Noor's beard, left his chair, and went toward the other end of the cell where Noor could make out the dark smudge of a door against the faded and pockmarked once-white wall. The door had been opened by someone on the other side, and now the inspector was leaning into an opening wide enough for his head and neck. Sounds of his conversation with the man on the other side of the door reached Noor, muddled voices from the end of a tunnel.

The door opened wider and the other man stalked in. After lingering by the door with the inspector, the two of them approached Noor, and he saw the prophecy of the inspector coming true, that he would, as threatened, be killed and confined to the afterlife in this tomb.

"This kind of thing, Salauddin? Again?" said the other man, looking down at Noor. "After all the warnings we've been receiving?"

"What am I supposed to do?" the inspector said. "Take him to bed with me? Fuck warnings. Let them come and do the job I have to do and then give warnings."

"Just look at him."

"Don't be fooled."

"I'm seeing with my own eyes."

"Then get out of here so you don't tax your vision."

"Mind your tongue, Salauddin. And someone get this man some water. Now."

Sometime after the other man blustered out of the room, a constable touched a tin cup to Noor's mouth. The water was warm and grainy but soothing as ice going down his throat.

"Enough," the inspector barked at the constable. "Take his hands down."

Rahim and Abdul brought him down from the back of the police jeep like they were unloading a medium-size piece of cargo. Noor's body unwound for the first time since being in the cell, no longer needing to strain every worn-out bone and muscle to stay upright or fight the tearing pain in his shoulders if he momentarily relaxed against the pull of the rope. In seconds he was unconscious.

Noor slept for three days. The others took turns keeping watch. They moved their card game to Noor's room, agreeing to play more quietly than their usual selves, but loudly enough for him to know they were there. Even Hashem Mia's memory set aside its idiosyncrasies, and he played each hand as a docile gamesman, relenting in a dispute and accepting the correction of the others. Late on the first night, as they were breaking up the game, Hashem Mia volunteered to take the first shift, and while

Rahim and Abdul wrapped up the game, stood over Noor and wept.

"We started work in this house the same week," he said. Then he drew the covers up to Noor's chin, and sat down on the ground at the foot of the bed.

In his sleep, Noor often shouted, sometimes a fearful scream, sometimes the fragment of a word. After the first few hours, the others grew used to it enough that the intervals between them began to be of concern. Sounds of any kind, at least, meant that he was still alive.

On the third day he awoke at dawn, just as Abdul was rising from his watch by the muezzin's call to wash for morning prayers. Noor was trying to pull himself up onto his elbows, moaning and grunting, barely able to raise his head a few inches off the pillow before collapsing again. He mustered up the strength to call Abdul's name and ask for water.

"Damn fool of an old man," Abdul chuckled with some relief. "I don't know how much longer I could have gone on with this."

They brought him food, which he feebly picked at and set back down.

"I have to get back to work," said Noor.

"Walk first, then worry about work," Hashem Mia placed a hand on his shoulder.

"What are you people eating?" Noor asked.

"The finest of Gulshan's roadside offerings," said Abdul. "Too good to last in your miserable stomach for more than five minutes," he laughed.

Noor was awake late into the night of his first day of consciousness, and Rahim sat with him, studying the cook's hollowed out face as Noor stared for hours out the window, his eyes still as stones.

"What did they do, Uncle?" Rahim asked.

Noor's head turned slowly to face Rahim for a second and returned to the window.

"Uncle, the man we work for has a big name and influence," said Rahim. "I promise you he won't be happy when he comes to know about this, and he will call friends who can do something."

"I need to use the bathroom," said Noor.

Rahim stood to help him, but Noor brushed his hand aside.

"A man who can't walk himself to the bathroom shouldn't be alive," he said, making a guttural groan as soon as his feet touched the ground and he placed on them the first hint of weight. Again, Rahim's help was rejected. The swollen balls of Noor's feet forced him to tread on his heels. Rahim followed Noor, keeping his distance, watching as pain shocked the cook's body with every step until he had descended the stairs, and disappeared around the back of the servants' quarters toward the latrine.

The entrance of a police jeep for the second time in two weeks tightened every muscle and tendon in Rahim, Abdul, and Hashem Mia, and every man was relieved that Noor Muhammad was not awake for it.

A lone inspector stepped out, not the same one as before. His build was slight but his uniform, tapered around his shoulders and arms, drew the movement of muscles that were ready for work. He walked with an urgency that was not rushed. There was even the trace of a smile, most evident in the corners of his eyes, as he faced the three men, one hand relaxing halfway in a pocket, the other reaching up every few seconds to smooth along the buttons of his tunic. In the late afternoon sun, his face shone from a fresh shave.

"Where is the man who was arrested?" he asked, his voice respectful and somber, and when there was no immediate answer, he waited.

"I'm not here to make an arrest," he said. "Please tell me this much, is he well?"

Rahim shook his head. "No, sir. He cannot move properly."

"Has he been seen by a doctor?"

"No, sir."

"Where is he now?"

"Sleeping, sir. I can wake him if you want."

"Absolutely not."

"Sir, all he wants to do is sit and look out the window, and stay in his room," said Rahim. "He's only just started eating again."

"I'm a great admirer of your sahib," said the inspector. "I wish he still made films, but every man reaches a time when he must stop doing even the thing he's loved and lived for. When he returns, give him my regards."

He waited a moment before turning, sliding into the driver's seat, and turning the ignition.

"You people don't worry about any more police visits," he said, his face framed by the window. "Just make sure someone is always awake and do regular rounds of the property."

"Take him to a doctor?" said Abdul, fanning his hand of cards. "Easy for the police to go anywhere anytime."

"We should," said Rahim. "I don't know why we didn't think of it before. Who knows how they beat him in there?" He slapped his hand down. "Damn. We're idiots. The inspector was right. I don't have to be a doctor to know that it's not natural for a man to sleep as much as he has been. Even if he is sick. Two weeks now. There'll be nothing left of him in another two weeks if it keeps going like this. I'm going to see if I can wake him."

"Right now?" said Abdul. "It's the middle of the night."

"Do you know a doctor worth his salt who won't see a sick old man in the middle of the night?" said Rahim.

"Maybe an old man," said Abdul, "not an old servant."

Rahim's chair scraped loudly as he pushed back from the table, stood up, and walked out.

Abdul and Hashem Mia persisted with their card game, speaking softly, absentmindedly, routine leading them from one hand to the next. Half an hour passed. Rahim hadn't returned. Hashem Mia's tea-burdened bladder needed release, and Abdul said he would take a walk around the house.

Both men paused outside Noor Muhammad's door. Rahim was on the floor, leaning against the edge of Noor's bed. Noor was lost to the mound of blankets and bed sheets, his form still.

Hashem Mia nudged Rahim to make him move out of the way, and then the gardener worked with great care to straighten and untangle every inch of the blanket and the bed sheet so that he could draw them, with a silent prayer, over the body of Noor Muhammad.

Acknowledgments

I'm grateful to these fine literary journals for first publishing the following stories: *Roanoke Review* ("Adulteress"), *East Bay Review* ("Dual Income"), and *The Milo Review* ("The Forced Witness").

My deepest gratitude to Chris Heiser and Olivia Smith for so warmly and enthusiastically welcoming this book at the Unnamed Press, and for the attention and care with which they gave it its US release.

Thank you to Pushpita Alam and Khademul Islam, under whose expert, supportive, and discerning guidance, this book was first published as *Days and Nights in the City* by Bengal Lights Books in Bangladesh.

Before that it was a manuscript sitting snugly on my computer's hard drive, surrounded by its family of other manuscripts. I wrote the stories that became this collection somewhere between 2012 and 2014. It wasn't until 2016 that I made the first contact with the person who would bring the manuscript out of my computer's hard drive and turn it into a book. K. Anis Ahmed liked the collection immediately and asked if I'd be interested in publishing it in Bangladesh. I'm endlessly grateful to him for being its first champion, and a continued supporter of my work.

About the Author

Nadeem Zaman is the author of the novel *In the Time Of the Others* (Picador India, 2018). His fiction has appeared in journals in the US, Hong Kong, India, and Bangladesh. He has a PhD in Humanities with concentrations on fiction and postcolonial studies from the University of Louisville. Born in Dhaka, Bangladesh, he grew up there and in Chicago. He lives in Maryland and teaches in the English department at St. Mary's College of Maryland.

@unnamedpress

facebook.com/theunnamedpress

unnamedpress.tumblr.com

www.unnamedpress.com

@unnamedpress